MW01146834

xoxo
the
Storm

# Taboo
## By Hilary Storm
### Copyright © 2016 Hilary Storm

## Kindle Edition

All rights reserved. Except as permitted under U.S Copyright Act of 1976, no part of this publication may be reproduced, distributed, or transmitted in any form or by any means, or stored in a database or retrieval system, without the prior written permission of the publisher. This is a work of fiction. Names, character, places and incidents are either the product of the author's imagination or are used fictitiously, and any resemblance to actual persons, living or dead, business establishments, events or locales is entirely coincidental.

Cover Design: Designs by Dana

Printed in the United States of America

## Dedication

To those not afraid to fall in love!

Taboo is a story about love. Love isn't always simple. In fact, often it's extremely complicated. Sometimes it's taboo and you have to decide just how much you care what other people think.

# Taboo
# Chapter One
# Noah

"How many fucking people are in my house, Levi?" He can barely hear me as I yell at him through the phone and try to get him to hear me over the background noise.

"Man, I've got us a few newbies tonight, just wait till you see the ass and tits I have lined up for us." Damn him. The last thing I wanted was a house full of temptation tonight. This new ink and the irritation of sitting all damn day have left me in a shitty mood.

"Levi. You're a dick."

"Aw, you know I got you. I'll even let you pick first."

"You're fuckin' right, you will."

"Get your ass here before I change my mind." He hangs up on me and I start my truck to get home as quickly as possible. I need to make sure they're not tearing up my damn house.

He has to find a place soon. I can't deal with this shit every night. He lets too many people through the doors and my house is getting torn up. When I throw a party, it's precise and only the best of the best are invited. He just tosses shit on the bar and cranks the music then calls it a party, inviting any piece of ass he runs into that day.

I'm still thinking about all of his bullshit when I shift gears harder than I mean to pulling onto my street, and that even pisses me off. *Fucking Levi.*

I pull beside the driveway and begin cursing out loud. Someone parked a topless Jeep in my fucking parking spot. I should have that piece of shit towed. The sound of music starting up and the vibrating of the windows pull my attention away from the driveway and directly into the window of my living room.

There are about twenty people that I can see, mostly women. I glance around to look at the rest of the cars and trucks parked on my grass and all down the street. Shit. I'm obviously not seeing nearly enough people in the window to account for all of these vehicles.

I open the door and it's like a damn deja vu. This is the kind of shit I did in college. Alcohol everywhere. Tits and ass everywhere. Loose women ready to do anything to make it to the bedroom hanging all over the few guys in the room.

"Noah! Look who I met today on campus." My eyes move to hers. I know those eyes.

"Kali?" Her eyes fall. The look of disinterest is noted. Levi begins walking toward me, leaving the three women behind. She's one of his trio. Fucker always picks three. It's a guarantee he'll get pussy. Hell, most of the time it means he's getting at least a threesome.

"Yeah, it's Kali. Look at those tits, man. She's grown the fuck up."

"Dude. Shut up."

"Aw, it's not like she's your sister anymore."

"I don't need you telling me what she is." She turns away from me and starts talking to a group of girls, acting like I'm not standing right here watching her every move.

"She's my pick." I lay claim to her before he has the chance to put his hands on her. Levi is a friend of mine, and that's the reason I want him to stay away from her. I know exactly how he is.

"No fucking way." He starts to walk away like I won't stop him dead in his tracks. I follow him, keeping my cool, for the meanwhile anyway. He stops near where he was standing before and I move in close to his ear.

"It's not fucking negotiable. Touch her and I will gut you." The cocky fucking smirk on his face goes all over me. He begins to stare into my eyes before I turn to leave the room, grabbing the bottle of Jack from the coffee table as I walk past.

Every room in my house is filled with people and shit is starting to already get trashed. What little patience I had before I walked into this house exits my body when I slam the back door. Maybe the night air will keep me from killing him.

She looks different. She's not supposed to look like that. It's been a few years since I last saw her and that night was a disaster.

I tip the bottle back and feel the liquid burn my insides. Trying to block these feelings, I continue to down the liquid fire, knowing it will only help me get through this night. If nothing else, it will make me not give a shit about anything. It's like I'm calling out for that idiot I've been trying to outgrow to come to the surface.

I sit near the fire pit, listening to the water from the waterfall as it hits the pool. It's starting to feel peaceful out here, even though I can hear the noise inside. It's not long before I can feel the effects of the alcohol, which I welcome.

I pull my shirt over my head to look at my new chest piece. It's sore as fuck, but exactly what I wanted.

The sound of the door opening pulls my attention toward her. She closes it behind her, stepping out onto the patio to talk on her phone. I just watch her as she moves in those heels.

"He's here." *Who's here?*

"Yeah, just come and get me. I shouldn't have come. I knew Levi would lead me to him, but I guess he's not interested." *What in the fuck?*

"Just text when you get here." She lowers her phone and starts to go back inside. I don't stop her. She needs to get the fuck out of here and now is the perfect time.

Seeing her is getting to me more than I want to admit.  She's always been a sore spot with me and that was before she literally turned into a woman that can steal the breath from my chest with just a simple look at her. *Fuck, when did she start looking like this? I need to get her the hell out of my mind.*

I slide my hoodie over my shoulders, leaving it open in the front before I take another huge swig of Jack and then go back inside. There's only one way to make her leave here and never look back. *It's time to fucking party.*

The second I step inside, a blonde moves in. It's as if she was waiting on me to return. This back room has cleared out, but I can still hear the party is going strong.

She runs her fingers inside my jacket and around my waist then presses her tits against me. I'm so fucking glad she's as short as she is because she misses the tattoo, just barely. Glancing over her head, I notice Kali has entered the room and is watching us. She's not upset at all and I need her to fucking hate me. I need her to walk the fuck away and never look back.

I slide my hand up the blonde's short skirt, grabbing ass and dipping my fingers inside her. Using the other hand to release her tits, I lower my lips to lick the fake perfection filling my hand. *She's still watching. I can feel her.*

The blonde's hands begin to open the button to my jeans and the feel of her grip on me has to be the reason I'm so hard. I refuse to believe it has anything to do with Kali watching me.

The blonde begins to kneel in front of me, exposing me even more to Kali. Her mouth around my cock feels warm and so damn good. It's instinct to wrap my hands in her hair and hold her close, that's the usual.... It's not normal for me to be looking into another woman's eyes the entire time I'm getting blown.

Someone walks into the room, causing Kali to turn and walk out. I don't even look to see who it was that entered, it's irrelevant. *Mission accomplished.*

I let the blonde finish me off; hell, she even swallows like a fucking champ. She tries to push for more, but honestly I'm not in the mood. I got mine; she shouldn't be such a whore, dropping to her knees so quickly.

"Nah, I'm good." I pull my pants up, leaving her standing there. She'll be pissed off, but I'm sure she'll get hers from someone else tonight. *A whore always does.*

I open the door to the rest of the house, glancing around to make sure she's gone. I don't see her, so I go upstairs to my bedroom. I'm over this night and all this fucking mess that Levi seems to get me in.

I send him a text to get everyone out of my house NOW. He'll take his sweet fuckin time, but at least this will get the ball rolling. I dial Mandy. She has to get her brother a place to stay tomorrow.

"What's up?"

"I need you to find this asshole a place. Tomorrow."

"What did he do?"

"Every fucking night is a damn party. I'm through with that shit. I like my house quiet unless I'm the one making the fucking noise." I lie back on my bed and sprawl out as she continues to talk.

"I'll see what I can find."

"It's only because he's your brother and we go way back that I haven't thrown his ass out already."

"And I appreciate that. I'll do what I can tomorrow."

"What're you wearing?"

"Noah.... You know I'm not going to play with you."

"Yeah. Can't blame me for trying."

"I've grown to expect it. How many are

there tonight?"

"My house is full of drunks."

"Go find you a piece of ass out there."

"I didn't see any that I wanted."

"I'm sure if you drank, you'd find someone that fits your standards. Especially since those standards change with alcohol."

"Hey now."

"You can't even deny it, Noah."

"Tell me how soft your tits are."

"Goodnight, Noah."

"COME ON."

"Noah, seriously. You know how fucking soft my tits are. You know they're a full-size D, and you know exactly how it feels to run your tongue over them."

"Keep talking."

"NOAH. I'll see you tomorrow." I hear the line go silent. Why do we have to be so good at fucking and so terrible at relationships? I've known Mandy since high school, and Levi is her twin.

She's always had her shit together,

whereas Levi is obviously a different story. That's exactly why I've spent more of my life chilling with Levi, but things have changed. I'm not ready to go backwards in life where my house is constantly trashed and the cops are called just to keep the noise down.

# Chapter Two
## Noah

I lie there mostly in the dark and start to think about Kali. No matter how hard I try to switch my thoughts to, hell even Mandy, I can't help but stay focused on the way she looked watching me. There's no doubt in my mind that she was turned on watching me. I swear if it would've been another woman standing there like that, I would've walked away from the blow job and approached her just out of curiosity. Anyone who can handle that has to be a fuckin freak. Knowing the woman that I constantly think about is at that level... should flip me the fuck out, but damn it, it doesn't. It intrigues me.

I stand and remove my jeans, dropping everything to the floor. My dick is twitching back to life and I start to consider walking back out there to bring a piece of ass into my room to play for the night. I need to wash the last whore off of me first. In fact, a hot shower sounds damn perfect. I can still hear the party going strong, even though I told that fucker to end it. He has until I finish this shower and pull my pick for the night to get people out of my fucking house.

Tossing my phone on the dresser near the bathroom door, I glance at the picture of me with my dad that sits under the only lamp lit in the room. I'm almost positive that picture had to be that summer we moved away from Kali and her mom. I had just turned eight…. she would've been six. I remember being confused by what was happening. That summer was the beginning of the life I would come to know all too well with a drunken father that doesn't even give a fuck if his son eats. I haven't seen him in years and don't plan to see that asshole anytime soon.

I stop dead in my tracks right after I step into the bathroom. That silhouette caught my attention. I really need to get my head out of my ass and take notice of my surroundings. It wasn't until the bathroom light hit that corner of the room that I even had a feeling I was being watched.

I could let her off easily and just get into the shower, allowing her to escape…. but what's the fun in that?

Instantly opening the door and taking a step back, I begin to move around the room. She's standing now, frozen in mid step, but I don't let on that I see her.

*What the fuck is she doing in my bedroom?* This shit is getting out of control. It's one thing for my mind to be thinking of her, but for her to keep showing up in my actual fucking space... that's a different situation altogether.

My anger starts to spark thoughts of how to handle this and I quickly choose to teach her a lesson. She should've never walked through the front door of my house, let alone the fucking door to where I sleep.

Grabbing a pair of shorts, I walk to the door on a mission as I step through each leg. This is a moment I'm going to say a silent thank you to Levi for being a pain in my ass and not listening about getting everyone out quickly because I can still hear the crowd. Turning the light on and leaving the door open, I step out into the hallway.

There's a hot brunette walking down the hall toward the room Levi is currently staying in.

"Hey." She turns her head with a sexy over the shoulder look and stops in her tracks at the sound of my voice.

"Oh, hey." Her hands go to her long hair as she starts to twirl one finger through a few strands.

I don't take a step out of my doorway, there's no fucking way I'm letting the person behind that silhouette escape before she gets an eye full of why she needs to stay the fuck away from me.

"Come here." The brunette turns and walks her sexy ass straight toward me. Her legs go on for days in those heels and that short red dress. Each of her steps is directly in front of the last, causing her hips to move with perfection. Shit, this will be such a perfect lesson for Kali.

"What can I help you with?" Her eyelashes have to be fake, they're too perfect not to be.

"Tell me you have a friend that you can bring to my room to join us."

"What exactly do you have in mind?" I move slowly toward her mouth, looking deep into her eyes. I let my hand slide up her small curves, purposely brushing every inch of skin my hand can cover. Slowly slipping my fingers into the hair covering the back of her neck, I grip tightly, pulling her head back with the force of my action. Her eyes widen and she begins to smile.

"You know what I'm after, go find someone." I drop my hand from the grip of her hair and turn to go back into my room.

She's moved from the frozen state she was in earlier. I don't see her right away. If it weren't for the fact that I noticed my closet door was closed earlier, I'd have no idea that she was still in here.

I purposely open the closet door all the way and turn on the light, before I toss my dirty clothes on the floor just inside. Remaining nonchalant is entertaining to me. I should really be nice to the girl I used to call my sister, but that ship sailed a few years ago.

A nice guy would never do what I'm about

to do.

The brunette didn't disappoint. Now I'm trying to decide who I should start with. There's a blonde with fake tits and golden brown skin, a red head with fair skin and from what I can tell a very nice set of real tits, and then of course the brunette I met in the hall. I honestly couldn't have chosen them better myself.

All three are half dressed to start with, not that they didn't enter the room sliding their straps down and their shirts off.

I'm deliberately standing with my back to the closet. If Kali is watching, she's got my naked ass as her view with my hand sliding up and down my dick as I try to prepare for this little show.

The girls begin to touch me, not leaving each other out in the process. It has to be their nails sliding across my skin that's bringing this chill to the surface. Although I do love the thought of someone watching me, in the past I always made sure everyone was in on the action. This time that will be different. She'll be watching.

I'll feel her eyes on me as I fuck these women and try not to think about her. The woman I used to live with as a child and considered a sister. *What kind of fucked up shit am I doing?*

I let the thoughts of my actions run through my head while at least two of them drop to their knees. Turning sideways, I give her a better view and the feeling of her watching hits me deep. My dick becomes rock hard knowing she's seeing this and I hate myself for wishing it was her mouth full of my dick. Her tongue running under the full length and giving me that moan of appreciation when she realizes just how long and wide my big dick really is.

Hands are everywhere. I don't have to do a thing. They all know what to do. I stand there with my legs just far enough apart for them to suck on my balls as well. This is a bonus for me. Very few women will put balls in their mouth.

The blonde moves to the bed with both hands pulling me along with her. I let her lead me knowing how this will go. I will fuck all night long. I will hit every angle of each of these women and hold my release until I can barely stand the thought of friction on my dick. This is how I used to do this and until now I didn't think I would want to ever do it again.

I reach for a condom and slip it into place. Getting a view of all the pussy I'm about to fuck, I stand and begin to contemplate this entire thing.

This is a dick move. I know this. She should be walking out of here and not tolerating my shit, yet from what I can tell she's still in that fucking closet hiding as if she's not here.

The women begin to lick and kiss and finger fuck each other. The liquid sounds of smacking in the room fills my ears. *Wetness.* So much fucking wetness at my disposal.

I dip my fingers deep into the brunette. Pulling her moisture out and leaving it all over her, I let my fingers slide up and down the crack of her ass.

She arches her back and tilts her ass to give me the best view of her in all her glory. So pink inside, so perfectly waxed on the outside. There's nothing prettier than that right there.

Lowering my face, I begin to taste where my dick will be sliding very soon.

I use my hands to lift her hips and spread her open, right before I tongue fuck her. My teeth grip her clit and tug, causing her to scream out as my teeth slide over her clit until it slips from my grip.

Glancing up as I make long strides with my tongue, I catch a glimpse of Kali moving out of the closet. I let my head turn to fully see her face and it's full of disgust. She's slow stepping toward the door trying to leave without a sound, but I need to make a point.

I move quickly toward the door, meeting her just as she reaches it. Her eyes won't meet mine. Her breathing is heavy and her chest is practically bursting out of her shirt. I'm not sure if it's her heart beating, her being turned on, or a combination of both.

She reaches for the knob and I raise my hand over her head to secure the door closed. She's facing it now, head lowered. My naked body gravitates toward her as I try my hardest not to smash her against the cold door and grind on that beautiful body. My dick is reaching for her. Our breaths begin to come simultaneously and I close my eyes before I say these words.

"Why is my sister trying to watch me fuck?" My voice is deep. Grumbly and breathy.

"I'm not your sister."

"Would your mom agree?" She doesn't respond but lowers her head even further. Her hand slides behind her and over the skin that's screaming to touch her. So close to the dick that's practically begging for her. I want this touch. I want to feel her grip, her nails to leave marks so I'll have the memory of her being there. But I can't.

"Kali. You used to refer to me as your brother. Stay the fuck out of my bedroom."

"Or what? You know I'm not the only one feeling like this." She turns to face me. Looking close into my soul, too fucking close to the depths of my thoughts as she moves me closer to her. My naked body is touching hers. Her hips against mine, I lower my forehead to hers and share her air for a few moments of breathing. My arm is still holding the door above her head, but I can't get enough air like this. I'm suffocating.

I pull my eyes away from hers and back away. Her touch is instantly missed.

"Kali, you'd just be another piece of ass. I'd rather not have to live with the fact that I fucked someone I called my sister."

"We aren't even related."

"Family isn't defined by blood. I will never fuck you."

"I miss you, Noah." *I miss you too.* I can't say this to her, I need her to leave before my internal strength gives in to what I really want.

"Kali. You need to get the fuck out of my house. I don't want you to come back. Just like I told you years ago, this will never happen." Dropping my hand from the door, I turn and walk my naked ass away from her. I'm thinking being naked isn't probably the best way to have that conversation. *God damn it.* I should've just thrown her out when I saw her in my bedroom at first. But I had to go and try to prove a fucking

point that she needs to stay away from me....
And then I end up plastered up against her body,
wanting to be deep inside her.

"Yeah, I remember.... It's taboo. Off limits,
against the rules. Take care, Noah." The sound
of the door closing stops me in my steps, she's
gone again. I see the three women on my bed,
licking and fucking as if I weren't even missing
from their equation. How is it I was able to tune
this out when I was with her? This is every man's
dream. Every man but me.

"Get the fuck out."

# Chapter Three
## Noah

This night will never end. I finally kicked everyone out of my house; well, everyone except the whore with Levi. The sounds of fucking coming from his room are my last straw.

I grab my sweat pants and put on my running shoes. Hopefully a run will help me get rid of some of this aggression. To be honest, I should've fucked those women. I should've fucked them so hard that I had no choice but to sleep.

I hear Levi bringing it home just as I close the door. Someone got special treatment tonight; he's not usually the type to give out multiple moments worth screaming over. I know this from years of being near his fucking ass while he gives no fucks about who is in his vicinity. When he wants to fuck... he fucks.

The streets are dark and the air is heavy. The weight on my shoulders is making me move slower than normal. Why the fuck does she insist on coming near me? Yes, it's taboo. Yes, she's off limits. Yes, that's disgusting to fall in love with someone you know as a sister. I'll always love her, but I can't handle her near me. My mind and heart aren't on the same page when it comes to Kali. I can't let my dick break the tie because I know where that'll end.

She couldn't grow up fat and ugly... no she's fucking sexy and sadly, doesn't even know it. I've stopped myself many times right before a slip of telling her just how beautiful she is. I've replayed one specific moment from high school no less than a million times.

She was broken. Some dickhead boyfriend of hers was fucking a cheerleader whore after a game. She was in her car crying in the parking lot when I walked by, so I stopped to check on her. She wrapped her arms around me and cried into my chest. I held her through her tears, not caring who was watching. I remember her relaxing when my hand slid down her back. She held me tighter, almost like she didn't want to let me go. I let the night air wrap us until there wasn't a single person left in the parking lot.

She finally pushed away from me just slightly, not wanting to look me in the eye; she kept her head lowered. Using my fingers to lift her face and my thumbs to dry her remaining tears, I moved her face until it was lined up with mine.

Time froze. My morals and my give a fucks went out the window as I stood and held her. I could see her thinking and she was struggling with what was happening more than I was. Her tongue sliding over her lip was the last test on my restraint. Leaning forward, I let our lips meet. It was slow at first, like we were making sure we weren't going to be zapped straight to hell for what was happening between us. Our tongues met even more shyly, then it was like a craving passion overtook us both. I couldn't get deep enough into her mouth, into her arms, into her space. I wanted to be everywhere and I couldn't get there fast enough.

My hands moved under her shirt; she slid her hands under mine. We knew each other so well, but this was us exploring each other for the very first time. Her skin was so soft and I hate that I can practically feel it on my fingers right now.

I stop running, gasping for air and fighting for a breath so hard that I have to bend and place my hands on my knees. The sweat from my head rolls down my face and over my eyes so I decide to walk what's left of my path back to my front door. Thinking about that night. Thinking about how I'm still to this day thankful I stopped that from going where I wanted it to. How she held on tight hoping for more and listening to her tears again as I knew I was breaking her even more than that dickhead she was seeing.

The next day was brutal. Word got out that we had that moment in the parking lot. That dickhead was trying to justify his actions to everyone, so he went public with a phone picture of Kali and me. Luckily it was just me holding her and we were able to keep the truly private moment exactly that.

Stepping into my kitchen, I smell coffee.

I'm gonna need coffee to get through this day. Levi doesn't drink it, so I'm sure it's his whore that's actually up and around. I don't feel like dealing with the awkwardness of meeting whoever it is in the kitchen, so I grab a cup and pour quickly. I hear the door to the pantry just as I finish topping off my cup.

I grab a hand towel from the drawer and turn, hoping to escape without being talked to. My grip tightens on my cup when I see her. She's wearing a black t-shirt of Levi's. She may or may not be wearing underwear underneath. Her hair is so fucked. She has 'fucked all night' hair. It hits me in that moment that it was her screams keeping me up. It was her in the bed that was slamming into the wall of my bedroom *all goddamn night.*

My squeeze is no match for the coffee cup in my hand as it shatters in my grip. Hot coffee explodes all down my body and all over the floor.

"FUCK." My skin screams in pain as the liquid runs through my clothes. I rip my pants down and my shirt off, trying to keep the heat of the coffee from burning me even further. *It's so fucking hot.*

"DAMN IT!"

"Shit, Noah. Are you ok?"

"Fuck no." She wets a towel and starts patting down my knees and thighs. She's kneeling in front of me when Levi enters the room.

"What's all the yelling?"

"The fucking coffee cup broke."

"Shit, man, I'm sorry."

"Shut the fuck up. I want you out of my fucking house now. You need to grow up and get your own damn place."

"Whoa. I didn't pour coffee on you, asshole."

"No, but you have done nothing but fuck shit up since you moved in." She stands and moves away from me, kicking my pants over my tennis shoes, which only pisses me off even more.

"Is this because I fucked Kali?"

"Don't fucking say that to me again. You

can fuck her all you want. Apparently, she has no respect and doesn't have a problem fucking your nasty ass."

"Noah, stop." She steps forward with hesitation.

"Fuck off, Kali. You shouldn't even be here."

"Look, I'll let you talk how you want to me, but leave Kali out of this." Levi interrupts and only sends me into a deeper rage about this entire situation.

"Oh, now you act like you respect her. How many years have I heard how much you'd like to fuck that ass of hers? About her goddamn tits? This is a girl that was once a sister to me, you fucking dick."

"What does it matter? You threw me out last night. You. Threw. Me. Out. Before you fucked your own whores. I'm leaving. I'm not going to put up with this shit from you, Noah. I can fuck who I want. I can be who I want. You want nothing to do with me, remember?" She's stomping out of the kitchen when Levi steps closer to me.

"Look, I can tell you fucking love her. I shouldn't have taken her to bed, but I won't apologize for it. Because it's making you see red right now. Maybe now you'll fucking quit worrying what everyone thinks and grab that one thing you're missing in life." Kali is fumbling with her things as she walks back in. Her clothes are twisted as she tries to straighten them. Levi stops her and brushes the loose piece of hair out of her face and I have to look away for a brief second before I find myself watching again.

"I had a great time last night. Let me know when you want to do it again." His words are deep, with that smooth way he talks to women he's trying to reel in for a fuck. She leans into his hug and kisses his lips with a quick peck. *What in the fuck am I watching?*

I watch them both leave out the door and I torture myself even further by moving to the window and following them down the driveway. I finally see her going to that piece of shit Jeep that's parked in my spot. *I should've fuckin known that was hers.*

She gets in and starts up the engine. I can see him lean in for another kiss, so I turn to walk away. *Walk the fuck away before I kill this mother fucker.* He has no fucking right to her lips. To her body. To touch her where I want to be touching. I swear I'll gut him if he even thinks this will ever happen again.

I hear the door slam just as I enter the living room. He's in the kitchen running water before I meet him again.

"Levi, get the fuck out of my house."

"Noah, cool your shit. I have to find a place first."

"That's just it, you've been told so many fucking times and you're not even looking."

"I'll look today."

"You're fucking right you will. I want you out by tonight."

"I can't find a place in one day. I need at least a week."

"You have three fucking days."

"I could always go stay at Kali's for a few

days."

His words make me irate. I can't stop myself from the urge to dive across the gap between us and grab him by the neck. My fingers are squeezing his neck when he punches me in the side and now it's fucking on. I'm filled with so much rage that I can't see clearly. It's as if it's all a blur and I'm just acting on chaos and insanity. We both keep landing hits that are meant to hurt badly.

I finally get some leverage and get him in a choke hold. My arms have him locked so fucking tight and his fingers scrape my forearm when he tries to get me to release. I squeeze tighter. What the fuck has happened to me in the last twelve hours?

He elbows me in the ribs and I finally let go.

"What the fuck?" He's gasping and trying to catch his breath and I watch him with barely any regard.

"I'm fucking done, Levi. I warned you. Don't you ever touch her again."

"Aw but see, Noah. You have no claim on her." He's bent holding his knees as he looks up at me, speaking through big breaths. "That's on you."

"The fuck I don't. Levi, I swear to you... I will cut you from your ass to your throat if you so much as touch her." I slam him into the wall, forcing him to stand and face me. We look eye to eye for a few seconds before he gives me a slight nod of acceptance.

I push off of him and begin to walk to my room. His words hit me as I turn the corner.

"Noah, when are you going to fucking do something about her? I've watched you live unhappily for years." I keep walking. He has no idea what he's talking about.

# Chapter Four
## Kali

I should've known not to go over there last night. I miss him. He was my person. He was the one I went to when my life got complicated and he always knew what to say. It's been years since I've seen him and I just wanted to make sure he was all right. I mean I've heard he's very successful, and by the looks of his house, he's doing well for himself, but I needed to see it for myself. Maybe I had some slight hope he would be happy to see me. Hell, maybe even missing me too.

The revenge sex was probably uncalled for, but I didn't want to go home alone after the shit I saw him do last night. He obviously has no respect for me and doesn't want me in his life. Levi just happened to be saying goodbye to the last guest from the party last night when I walked out of Noah's room. His arms felt nice. He made me feel like I was the sexiest woman alive and honestly for a moment, I believed him. He rocked my world with those position changes all night long. I feel like I've been fucked thoroughly. It's been a while since that's happened and it was long overdue, yet I feel like shit for doing it.

What's Noah's deal? He was so disgusted by me being there this morning that he got pissed at Levi for even touching me.

Stopping at a red light, I catch a glimpse of myself in the rear view. Nothing like the drive of shame in an open Jeep. I glance over and see the guy in the car next to me looking me up and down. I don't get a very good look at him because he starts to roll down his window and tries to talk to me.

"Hey." I try to ignore him, but he knows I can hear him without the top on.

"Hey, I'm talking to you." I turn up the radio in hopes of drowning out his voice just as the light turns green. We both move forward and he starts to pace me. I speed up in hopes of losing him, but he does the same. The next light is red too, so we have to stop again. He's a determined asshole.

"Bitch, I'm talking to you." He's getting louder. The song ends just as he begins to yell again.

"Look at me or I'm gonna teach you how to look at me when I fuck you again."

I slide on my sunglasses and try to hide the fact that my heart is racing out of control and my skin is crawling in dark memories. I know that voice now.

The light turns green and I slam on the gas pedal. Knowing he'll follow my actions, I hit the brakes quickly, making a quick left turn without slowing down very much. My Jeep begins to feel a little light on the left side as I make the turn and I immediately regret making this decision.

Time begins to stand still as my world starts to tumble. I'm trying to hold the wheel as the Jeep begins to slide. I'm jerked all to hell when I hit something and the Jeep topples over and over until it finally comes to a stop on the driver's side.

Reaching for my phone in the back pocket of my jeans, I pray to God that he doesn't try to get me. I unlatch my seatbelt and fall into the door, trembling as I try to think about where I am. I can't feel any pain through my heart racing as I hit redial on the last number called.

Levi.

"You miss me already?"

"Levi, I need you. Please hurry."

"Where are you?"

"Corner of First and Oak Tree."

"Are you hurt?"

"I don't think so. He's after me. I wrecked my Jeep."

"On my way. Stay on the phone with me, Kali."

"Please hurry."

"Who is after you, Kali?"

"Just.... Levi. Please fucking hurry. I can't talk about it right now."

"Kali, fucking tell me what I need to know before I get there."

"I hear a car. I can't talk right now."

"Damn it. I'm hurrying. Did you call 911?"

"No."

"Fuck, Kali. Are you sure you're not hurt?" He's yelling. I know it's because he's scared for me, but I can't take it. My adrenaline is in overdrive and I'm terrified as hell out here.

"I'm fine."

"Is anyone in there?" I hear a woman from outside the Jeep.

"Yes, I'm in here." She comes around until she can see me.

"I'm calling 911, they'll be here very soon."

"Thank you." Levi starts to talk to me again.

"Who was that?"

"A woman is here."

"911, we need help. A lady has flipped her Jeep and I see fluid running all over the ground. Please hurry." I can hear her voice getting quieter as she talks to the dispatcher. "Shit, Levi. There's fluid leaking from the Jeep."

"I'm almost there. Can you get out?"

"The Jeep is on its side. I can try."

"Are you sure you should move?"

"I think I'm ok." I put him on speaker and start to pull myself up from around the steering wheel. I'm feeling sore across my chest from the seatbelt and this is sure to be one hell of a bruise.

I can hear the squeal of tires just as I free my legs. "Shit, please tell me that's you."

"I'm here." His footsteps are pounding on the road just as I hear him say it.

There's liquid everywhere. I can smell gas as I finally start to get a grip on my surroundings. I'm just about to lift myself out of the passenger door when Levi scoops me up in his arms and runs from the Jeep. His strong body is an instant feeling of safety and I try not to be the typical damsel in distress wrapping my arms around his neck, but shit, I'm trying to support myself a little.

He's still running when I feel the blast. The heat from the flame surrounds us as I watch the inferno reach out and send us to the ground. He's somehow covered me with his entire body and we're face to face in what has to be a rock garden with grass growing through it. His eyes search for mine and he drops his forehead to rest against mine just as he locates them. His body collapses onto me when he sets his elbows next to my face and his arms around my head. His fingers get tangled in my fucked-up hair and I scream out in pain.

"Oh, shit. Sorry. Fuck, that was close." His breath across my face smells of bacon. This isn't quite as romantic as the movies, but right now in this moment, that bacon breath just saved my life.

"Damn, Levi. You're heavy."

"Shit, sorry. I guess I collapsed on ya." He rolls off of me and starts to look me over.

"Thank you for saving me." I try to sit and I wince from the pain I feel everywhere.

"You're going to the hospital to be checked out."

"Ouch. Shit, what am I on?"

"Well it's a shitty patch of grass and stickers. I'm pretty sure there's rocks too."

"Can this day get any better?"

"Well, I for one thought it started off great."
I ignore him as I move to stand. My Jeep has
rolling black smoke filling the sky overhead. The
sound of many sirens are in the distance. I look
for the woman and see her across the parking lot
walking, so I know she's ok.

As I move, I can feel the piercings of many
stickers across my back and ass. This is going to
fucking suck.

"Can you help pull some of these out?"

His eyes widen when he sees what he's
up against.

"Oh, baby girl. This is going to hurt."

"After the morning I've had, this should be
a cakewalk." He starts to pick out each sticker
one by one just as I see the fire trucks round the
corner.

"This is not how I pictured this day going."
I'm not sure how I had it pictured, but this is the
farthest scene from it. I watch as the firemen rush
to the Jeep and put it out in no time. Everything I
worked so hard for, up in smoke. My Jeep was
the first thing I actually had fully paid off on my

own. I probably should've kept that full coverage insurance.

# Levi

She has stickers everywhere. I haven't even touched the mess in her hair yet.

"Damn it. My Jeep!"

"I'm sorry this happened Kali, but at least you're not seriously hurt from what I can tell. That fuckin' Jeep can be replaced."

"Yeah, I know. Can you stay with me until the police get here?"

"I'm not leaving you. In fact, I'll be taking you to the hospital to have you checked out."

"Ok, just let me talk to the officer."

"Tell me who you were running from first."

"I promise I will as soon as this is all over. You can take me to my house after the hospital and I'll tell you everything. Just let me get this settled." I watch her limp her way over to the police car when it arrives. I figured she'd leave my house walking funny today, but this definitely wasn't in my game plan.

I hear my phone start to ring in the grass about five feet from where we just landed. Hell, I hadn't even noticed it wasn't in my hand yet. Kali does that to me. She always has. If it weren't for Noah, I think Kali and I would've tried to make something happen years ago. He's such an ass when it comes to her, though. She's 'off limits', yet he doesn't do anything about her. Well, I'm tired of fucking waiting on Noah to give me permission to do what I've wanted to for years.

The constant ringing interrupts my thoughts about the past. It's my sister.

"What's up?"

"Tell me you're looking for a place right now as we speak."

"Not exactly."

"Levi! Noah is pissed off. You have to start pulling your shit together."

"I got this. You don't have to worry, Mandy."

"Levi, you know you can move here."

"Nah. I'll figure it all out."

"All right. Please work on that partying

problem you have. It's not good for you to still be whoring around."

"Who says I'm sleeping around?"

"Please, I'm your twin. I know you better than you know yourself."

"What if I told you I found someone that may be worth trying to settle down for?"

"I'd call bullshit."

"Yeah, I know. That would be crazy."

"Do I know her?"

"Nah. I was just joking." Or am I? I'm seriously thinking about mentioning Kali, but Mandy would have my ass. She and I both know how Noah feels about her. I've definitely done a better job of keeping my feelings hidden than he has.

"Ok. Please try to find a place."

"I will when I finish what I'm working on."

"All right. I love you, Levi. When will I get to see you?"

"Maybe I'll take a road trip soon, you never know."

"I can't wait!" I see the officer questioning

Kali, so I rush off the phone.

"Talk to ya later, Mansy." I know she hates that nickname, but it wouldn't be a conversation with her brother without it.

"Bye, Levi."

"Bye." I start walking towards Kali. She's looking at her Jeep as the officer talks to her.

"I'm going to do some paperwork and I'll be back in a few minutes." He steps away from her as I walk up.

"What did he say?"

"Nothing, just asked me a few questions."

"Did you tell him about whoever was chasing you?"

"No, it wouldn't do any good."

"Why is that?"

"Levi, I told you I'll tell you later. Please just leave it alone." *Is she insane?*

"Kali. Fuck this. Do you see your Jeep going up in smoke? You need to get this guy on record."

"Yeah, well that didn't work so well for me last time, so I'll take my chances." I put my hand on her arm trying to comfort her before I start in on my reasoning, but she pulls away harshly.

"I'm serious. Not. Now." I can't imagine what has her acting like this. I can only imagine that I'm going to fucking hate what she tells me and I'm going to want to hurt someone if they fucked with her. The desperation in her voice when she called me has me so worried.

"Ok. I'll leave it for now, but like I said earlier, we will have this conversation today."

"Fine." She stops talking just as a few firemen walk over. The fire has been out for a while, but the smoke is still rolling from her Jeep.

"Ma'am, we have an ambulance headed this way to take a look at you, but I'd like to look at you myself before they get here."

"I'm fine."

"It appears that you rolled your Jeep. We need to make sure you weren't hit anywhere that may have caused internal issues."

"Ok." She looks like absolute shit, but this day has taken a big dump on her. I'm just not used to seeing her so rough.

I watch them look into her eyes and question her further. The ambulance finally gets here, but she turns it away. She's still stubborn as hell, just like I remember.

"Everything appears normal from what I can tell, but you should go to the hospital to be thoroughly examined." She gets the recommendation from the medic, but is shaking her head no before he finishes his sentence.

"I'm fine. Thank you for checking me over." She starts to walk toward me as soon as they hand her back her jacket.

"Please take me home. I need out of here." She talks to me as she walks past, headed straight for my truck. Her hair is a fucking nest of shit and stickers and on any normal day I'd give her hell about it, but not today. She looks like she's about to break and I'd hate to be the last straw that does it.

"I'll take you home, but I'm not leaving until you talk." I start the engine as I watch her rest her forehead on her hand as she leans against the passenger door. What happened to that confident woman that I fucked last night? The one so bold she ripped my clothes from my body the second we made it to my room.

The drive is quiet and she doesn't even look over at me until I kill the truck in front of her house. "He lives next door. I made the mistake of going on a date with him one time and then ended it. He didn't take well to my rejection and eventually I caught him watching me through my windows one night. He has threatened to make me fuck him again, but so far he hasn't done anything extremely aggressive."

"What the fuck, Kali? Tell me you have a security system in your house." I have to interrupt her because my insides are about to explode with anger.

"Yes I do, but you and I both know he can get to me when I'm not in the house. Plus, those things will only let authorities know he's already in my house."

"I'm giving you a fucking gun."

"I already have one. I carry it on me at all times." I sit back against my seat, not feeling any better about all of this. This guy sounds like a lunatic and I don't like the thought of her having to deal with him on a daily basis.

"You need to move."

"I plan to when my lease is up. The landlord won't let me out of my lease until it ends in three months. Until then, I have to stay because I can't afford anything else." My mind begins to think crazy thoughts, so I change the subject. Noah would kill me if I moved in with her, especially after last night.

"What happened today that caused your wreck?" It was something that occurred quickly after she left my place, so I'm worried he was stalking her.

"He started harassing me at a light and I turned so I'd lose him." She slumps in her seat when she starts talking about it all. My mind starts thinking about all the possibilities of things he's either done to her or plans to do.

"What did he say to you, Kali?"

"He just threatened me and I shouldn't have let him get to me because I fucked up my

Jeep and now I don't even have a way to work."

"I'll get you to work. But first I'm going to make sure this fucker never bothers you again. Which house does he live in?" I look around for any clue. None of the houses look like obvious psycho residences, not that I expected it to be spelled out across the fucking roof top.

"Don't do anything to make this worse. I'll be fine, Levi. Thanks for your help today." She opens the truck door and slides down to her feet. I race to meet her at the front of my truck and without hesitation I put her over my shoulder.

"There's no fucking way I'm leaving you here when some goddamn sicko is trying to get to you. Get your fucking ass back in my truck. I'm taking you to my place."

"Levi. Put me down!" She's screaming at me before I finish and using her fist to drive her point home as she punches me in the ass. "I'm fucking sore, you ass and don't you ever think you can tell me what to do." I set her down and wait for her to stop talking before I start.

"You're not staying here under any

circumstances. And if you try to, I'll be moving in with your ass. End of discussion."

# Chapter Five
## Levi

It's taking everything I have in me not to go over to that mother fucker's house and beat his ass as I witness how this is all tormenting her. She looks defeated and not at all the Kali I used to know. I'm still processing all of it as a car pulls into the driveway of the neighbor's house.

A dark haired, average looking guy gets out of the car and I watch his every move. His eyes instantly scan her yard and he strains to see inside my truck, no doubt being a nosy asshole. I hear her lower in the seat and know without asking that he's the one that's been fucking with her.

"So he just needs a reminder of how to treat people. I can handle this." I open my truck door and walk with a purpose to meet him in his yard. He takes a few steps back before I fully approach him. My guess is he saw the killer rage in my face that told him he was about to get fucked up.

Without saying a word, I punch him in his

face, taking him to the ground as I squeeze his neck, holding him in place. I connect every time my arm comes forward and it isn't until I hear Kali screaming at me that I stop. I'm breathing heavily and I don't release my grip because I haven't said the one thing I need to say.

"So much as look at her and I'll fucking kill you." He gasps for air under my hold and I finally release my grasp and allow him to breathe. "You're only breathing because I'm giving you permission to. Remember that." And with a shove, I stand to face Kali, frustration still flowing through my body.

He begins to huff out and spit blood while he crawls backward trying to get away from me, but what he doesn't understand is that crawling away from me won't save him. I'll ruin him for touching her and I won't think twice about it.

"Why did you do that?" She's looking around me to watch his pathetic attempt to stand while she questions me.

"Because I want him to know who he's fucking with." Looking down at my bloody fists before I start to walk toward her house makes me hate him even more. She follows me to her front door and I don't even have to ask to come in before she's guiding me inside and running the water over my hands in her kitchen sink.

My eyes brush over her face just as she looks up at me. Her soft hands slide over mine a few more times while we're locked into each other's stare before I purposely look away. "We look like two thugs who've had shitty fuckin days." It's easier to change the subject and work with her laughter than it is to deal with the way she was just looking at me. It's the way I've wanted her to look at me for years, yet she's never had eyes for anyone when Noah was around.

She turns off the water and begins inspecting my hands. "Looks like most of the blood was his. You have this one knuckle that's busted open. Let me wrap it for you." She leaves the room and comes back with some tape and before I have time to think about anything else, she's wrapped my hand to stop the bleeding.

She looks up at me when I use my other hand to brush the hair off my face. Our eyes lock again and this time I don't look away. I smirk just slightly and wait for her to react. It's time I stop denying what I've always felt for her and let this happen if she's ready to test the water to what we potentially have if we just give us a chance.

"Yeah, I think I'm going to jump in the shower and get some of this grass out of my hair." She takes a step back, never letting her eyes fall from mine. I take a single step forward and reply with the only response I've ever known when given this kind of bait.

"Maybe I should help you." She pauses and without any other response, she turns and leads the way.

## Kali

The heaviness he makes me feel when he looks at me like he does is something I'm not used to. I've never noticed how piercing his blue eyes can be, but maybe that's because I've never really taken the time to notice. Levi is... well, he's Levi. He's a mess and has never been someone that I'd ever consider fooling around with. I guess I always hoped Noah and I would eventually stop resisting what fate has in mind for us, but it's obvious after last night and this morning that he's not interested in anything that has to do with me.

I love Noah. But loving Noah means I've always had a respect and a tolerance for Levi. The way he has treated me since last night is more than I could've ever imagined. Sex with him is phenomenal and I'm honestly not going to keep it from happening again if he wants to take it there. I'm available in that department, it's just that I'm emotionally attached to the idea of what I thought Noah and I could have. No matter how hard I try to shake Noah out of my mind, he's there lingering and haunting me.

"Fuck, Kali. Why did we wait so long to do this?" Levi whispers against my ear as he pulls me against him from behind. I can feel his

erection bulging against my ass and he doesn't
hesitate to slide my shirt over my head and slide
both hands over my body. "Let me see you in
the light. Jesus, your skin is soft." His touch
sends a chill over me that feels very nice. One
that I haven't felt in at least two years. I swallow
hard while he strips me naked and begins to kiss
and touch every inch he can reach.

I'd never tell him that last night was my
first night to go to bed with someone in that long
because he'd think something was wrong with
me. I can't help that I chose to focus on my
education in hopes that one day I'd meet Noah
again and be able to show him that I am
someone worthy of his love. I shake my head at
my ridiculous way of thinking and try to get back
in the moment with Levi. The last person that
should be on my mind while I'm in Levi's arms is
Noah.

I lay my head back on his shoulder when
he slides his hands down the front of my shorts.
It takes no time for him to send me into a fury of
sensation that makes me look desperate and sex

crazed. He's drawn me to my tip-toes as I work through every circle of his fingers on my clit. I try to open my legs even wider to give him better access, but he pulls his finger out and I watch him in the mirror as he slips it between his lips. The steam from the shower leaves a slight haze, but I can still see everything he does.

He's staring at me with a carnal look in his eyes as if he's about to consume me and make me forget about everything all over again. Slipping my hand behind me and into his hair seems to make him move even faster to get my pants off of me. Before I have time to comprehend what's happening, he's lifted me onto the bathroom counter and he's standing completely naked between my legs. I look down at his cock and listen to his moan just as I slide my fingers over it. He stands proud while I slide my hand over him a few times, taking the moisture already seeping from the tip down his length.

A piece of grass falls on my chest and it catches his attention for a slight second before he leans over to pull a condom out of his pants pocket. "I'm going to need to buy a case of these fuckers with you around." *Me around?*

I push his statement from my mind when he thrusts forward, filling me quickly. "Oh, fuck. This position is going to kill my legs." He slams forward again into the cabinet before he lifts me into his arms and begins to fuck me even harder than he did last night. I've lost all thought and comprehension by the time he steps into the shower, taking me to the wall before he begins to move inside me again.

The hot water sends a path down my chest and over most of his body. He leans forward and the shift in position sends me into an instant orgasm that I don't even try to hold back. I've never been noisy during sex, but Levi brings it out in me.

He fucks me continuously into another fit of spasms and I catch him watching me as I come down from the last high. He's not looking at me like he's enjoying a casual fuck, he's watching me with something in his eye that feels like this is more than that to him. I shut my eyes and close off allowing him to see inside me like he was trying to and just let myself feel what he's doing to me.

"Let's wash this hair of yours before I take you to bed." He brushes the hair from my cheek before he sets me down on my own two feet and for the first time in my life, a man washes my hair. He's careful with his fingers in my tangled mess and when he's done making me feel like I'm completely cherished, he grabs my body soap and squeezes it over my chest.

His touch makes my body come alive with sensations that I'm not ready to feel with him, so I take over and rush through the rest of the shower. He must sense my shift because he snaps out of whatever soft crap he was trying to do and grips my hair in his hand and pulls me to face him chest to chest.

"If I want to wash your sexy body, you fucking let me." His bite on my bottom lip reminds me how he was last night. This is more like what I imagined Levi to be like in bed.

*This I can handle. No emotions. No feelings. Just fucking.*

He lifts me to straddle his waist again and walks us both out of the shower. "I'm about to fuck you senseless." In a few short steps, he's tossing me onto my back on the bed and climbing over me. The condom is long gone and he starts to cuss about not having another one nearby when he climbs back out of bed and gets one out of his pants.

He's back in position quickly and I'm throwing my head back as he enters me hard and fast once again. "Fuck, you feel great on my cock." He slows only long enough to roll over and pull me on top of him. He pulls me forward as I straddle him and he fucks me fast while he holds me in his arms. It's all happening so fast, I'm moaning again before he has a chance to finally get his own release.

Just as his body begins to twitch and our breathing is completely chaotic, there's someone beating on the front door. "Open up, it's the police."

We both freeze in place, looking at each other in shock even though I shouldn't be surprised. That asshole neighbor of mine must've gone to the police.

"Shit, Levi. What are we going to do?" He guides me off of him and rushes for his pants.

"We're going to tell them the truth." I watch him slide his pants over his ass and take a deep breath, dreading what's about to happen.

He sees me struggling and leans over the bed until he's face to face with me again. "If something happens and they take me, I want you to promise that you'll go to Noah. Tell him everything and he'll make sure you're safe."

"I can't do that. I'll be fine." The banging gets louder and they're getting more impatient the longer we're taking.

"Fuck no. I need you to do agree to what I'm saying before I open that fucking door." He pulls my chin until I can't hide from the glare in his eyes.

I have no choice but to agree when they begin to beat down the door. He moves quickly through the house and opens the front door while I rush around to get my clothes on. Before I can get out of my room, they have him in handcuffs on his knees while they're being rough with him. He's trying to answer their questions, but they aren't giving him the chance.

"I told you if you gave me another reason to bring you in that I'd make sure you get what you've had coming." The bald officer spews his words with hatred in his voice. Before I can get to him, another officer holds me back.

"You don't want to interfere with us, young lady. Have a seat here and we'll talk to you in a few minutes." He guides me toward the couch and pushes me down until I'm sitting. Levi watches and comes even more unglued.

*How did this day turn into such a disaster?*

# Chapter Six
## Noah

No matter how hard I try, I can't get her screams out of my head. I can't help but wish it could've been my dick that was making her come undone all night long. She looked so perfectly fucked this morning and even though I shouldn't care if she's with Levi, I fucking do.

I don't want to see anyone touching her and I sure as hell don't want to hear it. I'm still cleaning my house, with no sign of Levi for the entire day. I'm going to beat his ass when he finally shows his face around here. It was his party and somehow I end up doing all the clean-up.

My phone rings and I don't recognize the number, but I answer it anyway. "Noah. I'm in jail. Listen to me. I need you to find Kali and take her to the house until I get out. She's in trouble." Before he has a chance to say another word, I'm already out the door. I'm sitting in my truck before I realize that I have no idea where she lives.

"Where is she?"

"Corner of Oak and Chestnut. Her neighbor is a fuckin' ass and you have to get her out of there." The call is disconnected without any further information. I rush like an insane idiot to get to her house, only to get no answer when I knock on the door.

*What in the fuck?* "Kali, where in the fuck are you?"

I glance around trying to guess which house the asshole neighbor lives in, but there are honestly two options as I scan the area. This isn't the best neighborhood and I find myself frustrated that she'd live somewhere as unsafe as this.

Banging on the door one last time, I stand and wait for her to answer. She finally pulls the wooden door open and I don't say a word when she looks at me like she's had the worst day in her life. I open the screen door and step inside without waiting on her to invite me in. Her face is covered in tears and I try not to notice that she's only dressed in a t-shirt and tiny shorts.

"Why are you here, Noah?" Her words are barely a whisper, yet full of sadness and exhaustion.

"Levi called me. He says you're not safe here..."

"I'll be fine. I'm not your concern." She interrupts me before I even have the chance to invite her to stay at my house until we get to the bottom of what's going on.

"I'll fucking decide when you're my concern." She slams the wooden door closed before she locks the deadbolts and walks out of the room. I do what I've always done when she's been this way in the past. I follow her. Pushing the door open, I catch her lifting her shirt over her head. Her tits are looking even better than I imagined and no matter how much I want to turn around, I can't. She has me locked and frozen in place just watching her, even though she has no idea I'm in here.

"Damnit, Noah. You can't just walk in here like that."

"Right. We always let the other one know

when we've entered a bedroom. Should I remind you about last night?" I walk closer to her, knowing I'll never be able to touch her, but wanting to so fucking bad that I can almost taste her.

She pulls a tank top over her tits, without putting on a bra and that begins to fuck with my mind even more than seeing her naked did. Her nipples are hard, poking through the pink material and teasing me beyond belief. "We have to go get Levi."

"What is he in jail for? Maybe he needs a night in the slammer just to learn a lesson."

"He was protecting me. I have to get him out." She slides her arms through a jacket and pulls a pair of jeans over her shorts, no doubt opting to spare herself from me watching her naked ass while she moves around the room. A part of me is relieved about that, and the other part wants to grab her by the hair and tell her exactly what she should be doing with me in her bedroom.

*She's off limits. Remember that, you*

*asshole.*

"I'll get him out. You don't need to be at the police station. She looks over at me, almost frantic while I wait for her to fight me on this.

"I should go with you." She begins to rush around the room gathering a bag and brushing her long, damp hair.

"Sure as fuck didn't see the two of you hitting it off quite as hard as you have. Since when did you start liking Levi?" She stops mid stroke through her hair before she points it at me with a glare in her eye.

"You do not get to do this. I came to that party looking for you. You. Pushed *me* away." There's a quiver in her voice before she turns away to busy herself again.

"I know what I said. I still feel the same way as I did last night." She doesn't get to know what that truly means. I'll let her believe what I worked hard to make her see last night. No matter how tempted I am to walk over to her right now and pull her curvy body against me, I have to keep a distance.

"Let's get him out and then I'll leave you alone and never bother you again. I just don't have a car right now." She refuses to look at me and I don't force her to.

"What happened to your Jeep?"

"It broke down. Let's go. I don't want him there any longer than he has to be." She walks out of the room and opens the front door. I watch her lock three different deadbolts and that only adds to my list of questions that I'll have to ask before the night is over. "I see you still love your sports cars." She makes a quick comment before she opens the passenger door and slides in. I don't respond because she's right. It's my one vice in life. She doesn't need to know just how many I have stashed in my storage garage downtown.

The rev of the engine breaks the awkward silence in the car and it isn't until I look over at her that I see her attention focused on the house next door. It takes me a second to see the weasel sitting on his porch just watching us. "Is that the fucker that Levi was talking about?"

"Please don't do anything. Let's just go get him out and try to forget this day ever happened." I choose to listen to her only because I don't want to even think about going to jail at the same time as Levi and her being left out here with some fucker, especially when I don't even know the full extent of what has happened.

I do as she requests and I drive us both to the police station. When we arrive, she seems nervous and no matter how strong my instincts are to protect her, I simply open her car door and wait for her to stand next to me.

I've asked a bail bondsman to meet me here and it's reassuring to see him already working with the officers when we walk in. "He'll need to be present for his court date in two weeks." It's quickly obvious that Levi won't simply be getting a slap on the hand over what has happened and I'll have to find out what in the hell went on tonight. One look at Kali and I can see regret written all over her face as she takes in what's being said.

She stops a tear from falling down her cheek and I feel a twinge inside my chest that reminds me of the way I felt when I tried to protect her all those years ago. *I know I shouldn't want to kill someone for her hurting like she seems to be, but apparently, it's in my nature and something I'm never going to stop doing.*

# Kali

This day is never going to end. Being inside this place again just reminds me of the hell that asshole has gotten away with all these times. It makes me crazy to think he's turning this all around now and playing the victim when I've tried to get him taken in for being the creep he is and he always seems to slip through the system, no matter how many times I turn him in.

I'm to the point now that I have no faith that justice will ever be served unless something *accidentally* happens to him when he tries to come into my house again. If that's what it takes to make this end, then that's what I'll do.

I hate that Levi and Noah are now involved. The last thing I wanted was for Noah to find out and start trying to help when he's made it very clear how he feels about me. I can't handle him dipping in and out of my life and if he thinks I'm in danger, that's exactly what he'll try to do.

"Please wait in the lobby and we'll process his release." The young officer seems helpful now that there are two men here with me. It's amazing how different things are when you come with *friends.*

Noah pulls the bondsman to the side and they both talk quietly so I can't hear. I sit and take in everything that's happened today and wish like hell I could go back to yesterday and never go to that party. It appears to be the turning point that made everything in my life complete chaos.

"All right, get me the *fuck* out of here." I stand the second I hear Levi's voice. He looks at me instantly and the grin on his face may be misplaced in this situation, but holy shit I needed it. He walks over and wraps me up in his arms. His warmth is exactly what I needed and I don't even look to see if this is pissing off Noah. He can get over himself.  This isn't about him.

"Hey, baby girl.  I fuckin missed you."
Levi's voice rumbles next to my ear and I can
finally breathe knowing he's out.

"This is all my fault.  I shouldn't have
called you."

"Stop that shit right now.  I'd do it all over
again this very second if that fucker was in this
lobby."

"Please just take me home."  I know he
would, that's the problem.  I don't want him to
have to fight my battles.

"Not on your fucking life.  You're staying
with me tonight."  He takes me by the hand and
guides me out the door.  "Here, let's talk out
here.  That place makes me fuckin'
claustrophobic."

"I can't stay with you. Noah would kill us."

"He'll have to get the fuck over it, because
you're not staying in that damn house so that
asshole can just walk right over and get you
anytime he wants.  You'll never stay there alone
again and I'll make fuckin' sure of it if it's the last

thing I do." He starts pacing in front of me, running his hands through his messy hair while I listen to everything he says knowing he has a point, but the thought of dealing with Noah constantly makes my insides twist into a knot.

"Maybe I should just get a hotel room…" He interrupts me before I have a chance to continue.

"No. It'll be fine. Just let me handle it." Without giving me a chance to argue, he walks toward Noah as he exits through the glass doors. I don't have the heart to go near them; I can't stand the thought of listening to Noah deny him when he asks to let me stay at his house. He made it very clear last night and this morning that he did not want me there. I don't expect him to change his mind now.

I look around and it's already getting dark, but the urge for me to flee is overwhelming. I hate waiting on yet another disappointing denial from Noah and instead of doing just that, I start walking while the two of them talk. I can tell it's not going well by the way they're both animated in their responses.  Fuck Noah.

I don't want his help.  I don't need his help.  And the last thing I'll ever do is let him think I'm a helpless charity case that he needs to save.

I'm almost two blocks away before I hear the roar of his car engine.  Just like I expected, they drive by slowly, looking for me.  Hiding in a doorway was the only way for me to stay out of their sight.  I can still see the back end of Noah's car when my phone rings.

"Where the fuck are you?"  Levi sounds angry.

"I'll be fine."

"That's not what I asked you.  Where are you?"  The car continues down the road, so I step out of the doorway only to come face to face with Noah.

"Nice try, Kali. Levi, back track about a block.  We'll be waiting."  I hang up and walk with a heavy step away from him.  *He doesn't get to hate me and want to save me at the same time.*

"Since when do you track people on foot?"

"Since Levi stole my car and told me to find your ass." It's obvious he's frustrated by his rude tone.

"Look. I don't want to *inconvenience* you any further. Just take me home and you'll never see me again."

"Sounds like a perfect plan, but Levi tells me I need to hear some shit that will change my mind. So, I'm giving him the benefit of the doubt and told him we can take this conversation to the house. You can stay tonight. That'll give you a chance to figure your shit out." He walks past me and I can't tell if he wants to dismiss me or scream at me.

When Levi pulls up, Noah walks with a determined stride straight to the driver's door. "Get the fuck out of my car and if you do that shit again, I'll kill your ass." Levi steps out and gives me a glare that's telling me he's not happy with my little stunt. I ignore him and take the back seat, feeling defeat from this terrible day wash all over me.

*I just want to go to bed and forget*

*everything that's happened today.*

# Chapter Seven
## Levi

Damn her and that cute little ass of hers. Noah catches me watching her walk by while we wait for her to pack a bag at her house. I swear he practically growled at me, but I pretend to be oblivious to his behavior. He has pushed her away his whole life and I stood back because I thought he'd come around one day. He's made it very clear that he won't, so I'm not going to deny what I'm feeling anymore.

"This will be enough for tonight. I'll just come back tomorrow when I figure out where I'm going." I look at her, confused. What does she mean when she figures it out? She'll be staying with me until she can afford another place. If I have to move in with her to help her, then I will. I'm still not sure what Noah will do once he hears everything. He could be a dick and throw us out tonight, or hell, he may surprise me and say she can stay if she needs to.

Something tells me he'll decide she needs

to stay once he hears everything, though.

   The drive to our house is quiet until Noah starts asking questions. I tell him all about the events of the day and it seems to shock him into silence, which is something unusual for him.

   "You can't go back to that house alone." This is the first and only sentence he says in the car after I start explaining everything.

   When we pull into the driveway, Kali doesn't open her door right away. I can see how stressed she is about this day and it seems only right that I break the ice in a way that only I can.

   "Let's go for a swim. Last one in has to clean the bathrooms." I strip off my shirt and drop my pants on the front lawn. I turn back to look at them both and catch Noah nodding and looking down while Kali watches with her mouth wide open.

   "Are you out of your mind?" she finally laughs around her words.

   "I'm a fuckin' free man... and I want to swim. Come on." I take her by the hand and lead her to the pool in the backyard. Noah doesn't follow, but I didn't think he would.

"Levi, are you insane? You can't just walk around naked in the yard."

"I do it all the time. It'll be fine. Just drop the cotton, Kali. We need to cut loose and forget this fuckin' day." I can see her inner struggle as she tries to decide whether to say *fuck it* and skinny dip with me or pretend she's more conservative than this.

"You know you need to laugh and just live in the moment after this day, so start pulling those clothes off, before I do it for you." She shakes her head in disbelief and tries to walk to the house, but I stop her before she gets too far. Pulling her into my arms is easy. It feels right and she doesn't try to pull away as I hold her.

"Did you take it in the ass today?" She starts laughing before she finishes her question.

"Hell no. I went in there pretending I was an insane person. The others left me the fuck alone." I start to lift her shirt, but she steps away from me and does it herself. "Wait, go slow. Give me a little strip tease." She slows her pace, but walks toward the water as she removes her clothes, one piece at a time. Her tits stand perfect, moving slightly as she steps into the pool. I watch her body become blurred as she gets deeper into the water. My dick is hard before I even get wet, but the second I do, I'm on a mission to get to her.

She leans against the side of the pool and waits for me to get to her, her eyes never leaving mine as I watch her shift from being uncertain to deciding she wants this just as much as I do.

As soon as I'm near her, she wraps her legs around my waist and her arms around my neck. Her kiss is very aggressive and it turns me on even more. I don't have to worry about a condom with her; we already established that last night.

Sliding into her isn't easy, especially in the water. She rotates her hips until I'm inside her and I let her continue to ride me while I just hold her in my arms and kiss the hell out of her.

Her moans get louder, but never so loud that anyone else will hear, even though I wouldn't care if they did. I slip my finger between us and rub her clit until she's writhing through an orgasm and bringing me close to my own. I start to watch her face as she goes over the top and that sends me straight into a fucking fury. Or is it a fury of fucking? Either way, I begin fucking her so hard and fast that the water begins to splash around us as her tits float between us. The water even hits our faces a few times, but it never slows us down.

*I actually hate fucking in water, but shit, this time it was perfect.*

"Fuck, Kali. We're going to have so much fun together. I have a feeling you're a little freak." She kisses me while I try to catch my breath and speak to her at the same time.

"It takes a freak to recognize one." I try not to react to what I'm seeing behind her as she responds, but she catches the change in my face. She turns her head quickly and we both stare at Noah as he sits in a lounge chair drinking a cocktail.

*What in the fuck? Is he out of his damn*

*mind?*

I lower us both into the water to hide Kali from any further exposure. She's not happy that he's sitting there, which she makes obvious the second she opens her mouth. "Jesus, Noah. What the hell do you think you're doing?"

"Just having a cocktail and sitting by my pool. What else would I be doing, Kali?" His tone is condescending and even though I probably shouldn't have just had sex in his pool, I'm not going to put up with his moody bullshit tonight. If he blows this out of proportion, we'll just leave and get a hotel room.

"Can you at least toss me my clothes?" She leans up on the side of the pool in an attempt to get him to make this situation a little less awkward. Noah erupts in laughter. Not just a small chuckle, but full on hysterical laughter before he just suddenly stops and responds.

"No. If you want your clothes, walk your ass out here and get them. We've now all seen your fucking tits, so why not let the neighbors get a glimpse as well."

"Noah, you're being a dick and I knew I shouldn't have agreed to come here." She lifts herself out of the water from the side of the pool and gracefully walks to get a towel. She wraps herself in it before she bends down and gathers all of her things that are in a trail from the pool to where Noah is sitting. She says something to him just before she passes and then she walks into the house.

Well if that isn't a cock blocking moment, I don't know what is. "What the fuck is your deal?"

"Deal? What makes you think I have a *deal*?" He's even more intense and rude now that she's gone.

"Look, we'll just go get a hotel room. I didn't realize you'd be such a dick if she stayed here with me." I step out of the pool and walk through the patio area completely naked and soaking wet, not giving a shit who sees me or if it pisses Noah off even more. "I'll pack my crap and get us both out of here. Don't worry, you won't be bothered by us anymore."

# Chapter Eight
## Noah

*Us?* No fucking way am I letting there ever be a way for him to say 'us' and it refer to him and Kali as if they're in some sort of fucking relationship or something. Over my dead body will she end up with him.

"I told you that you could stay here. I didn't say you could just fuck each other out in the open like fucking animals. Have some damn decency, you asshole." He stops in his tracks at my response. I wait and hope for him to take a swing at me, because I want more than anything to beat the shit out of him and take out all of this built-up aggression on his ass. He's the cause of it all, so it only seems fair he's on the receiving end of it.

Instead, he doesn't say a word as he walks past me. Fucker probably knows I want him to initiate a fight and chooses to torment me even further by making me fester in my own agony.

"We'll move out tomorrow." The door

slams just as he stops talking, causing me to blink at the sound. I lift my glass and take back the last of my whiskey before I follow him inside.

The house is quiet and the only sign of either of them is the wet footprints tracked through the house that lead me directly to the front door. I open it and listen to the two of them argue and regret my asshole behavior instantly. I step onto the porch and stay out of view of them both.

"I'd rather stay at my own house and wait on that fucking rapist next door to try to come get me than deal with the weight of Noah's anger toward me. I don't get him and I honestly can't deal with this tonight. Levi, please just let me go. I'll be fine. I've been good my whole life without you guys, so I'm sure I can figure something out with this."

"You're out of your damn mind if you think I'm going to let you go back to your house with that insane person living next door. He's already tried to get to you and what he did tonight was just his way of getting to you again."

"Levi. He hates me with a passion. I shouldn't be here at his house and we definitely should *not* have just fucked like that in his pool. You make me crazy when you're around and it's just not fair for you to flaunt me around like you do. Noah and I are complicated and even though he will never feel the same way I do; I love that man. I don't want to see him hate me like this. If he has to hate me, it's easier for me not to have to face it. I need to go." I watch her try to walk away as she slides her shirt over her head, then she pulls her towel off and throws it at Levi. "Put this on and quit walking around with your dick hanging out."

He reaches out to stop her from leaving and they start talking so quietly, I can't hear them. I watch Levi take her in his arms and pull her close to him. She wraps her arms around him and leans into him as if he's actually consoling her. That should be me holding her like that, but instead I've made these fucking rules that I'm beginning to hate myself for.

When they begin kissing again, I go

inside. I can't watch the two of them go at it again, because I honestly don't think I can handle what it does to me. I know deep down I want it to be me that's fucking her. I want to feel her tits against my chest and watch her face as she comes undone, but instead, I'm the creep who was just watching in the background. I guess that's one that I owed her. I hope to never cash in on the other she was caught eavesdropping on.

I go to my room and flip on the stereo. Flopping down on the bed, I notice I have a few missed calls. One of them is from Mandy, so I hit that notification and wait to hear her voice, knowing not even hers will get Kali's out of my head.

"Please tell me everything is better. Did he find a place today?"

"No, he got tied up with some other things, but I'm sure he plans to take care of it soon." I choose not to tell her about the arrest or the fact that Kali is staying here. It's all too complicated and she'll just give me a lecture about shit I already know. "How is everything at your place? Is this call to tell me you're coming to see me? I can kick a bitch out of my bed if you want to keep me warm." If I tease her, she won't think anything is wrong with me because that's how I've always talked to her.

"No, I'm not going to keep you warm. Nice try, though. How about you change those sheets between your whores once in a while."

"I will for you." She has no idea how much different my life is now. When she was around, I was going through the party season of my life. I guess the last few times we've talked don't help my case in that, not that I'm trying to make one.

"I'll let you know. I was just checking to make sure you didn't kill my brother. He hasn't answered my calls or texts all day."

"He's been real busy helping a friend out." My insides twinge as I think about just how *much* he has been helping.

"All right. Tell him to call his sister tomorrow or I will make the trip to kick both of your asses." She hangs up before I have the chance to take the bait she just fed me. She knows I'm a sucker for that shit.

I lie back and force myself to doze off. Tomorrow can't come soon enough as far as I'm concerned.

My phone vibrates, waking me up. It's just an old hookup wanting a bootie call and I couldn't be any more uninterested. I glance at the time to find it's just after three o'clock in the morning. The stereo has covered any evidence that anyone else was in the house, so I'm not sure if they're here or if they ended up leaving. I guess I'll have to be fine with either option.

I toss and turn a few times before I give in and slide off the bed. Opening the door to my room, I step out and listen for any proof that either of them are still here. Levi's door is closed, so I can only assume they stayed.

Working my way downstairs to the kitchen, I hear someone moving around. It only takes one glance over the railing to see Kali mopping the floor in front of the door.

"Why are you mopping?" She jumps as I speak, but quickly returns her focus to cleaning the floor.

"Because I walked through the house and left footprints. I figured I should get them out before I leave." I take the last few stairs slowly as I watch her long brown hair sway as she moves. Her yoga pants and black tank top tease me when she takes the bucket and walks back to the kitchen, leaving me standing with only my fantasy of touching her. I follow her, intrigue forcing me to do what I wouldn't normally do.

"Look, I'm sorry if I woke you. I just wanted to clean up the mess I made. I promise I'll leave today so you can stop being angry." She closes the pantry door and attempts to walk by me. I put my palm on the doorframe, preventing her from leaving without talking to me longer.

"What makes you think I'm angry?"

"Because you feel heavy. I know you, Noah. And right now, you're not in a good place and I can only assume that it's me that's making you this way." She takes a step back, pulling her hair into a mess on top of her head with an elastic band from her wrist. I can't seem to pull my eyes away from her as she moves around the kitchen.

"I don't like the way Levi is with you." I admit what's bothering me and she stops suddenly, glaring at me as she takes in what I just said.

"You don't like him saving me from an asshole today. Him carrying me from a burning vehicle and softening my fall when it explodes. Or is it that you don't like that he went to jail fighting for me to be safe in my own house. Oh, I bet it's that you don't like that he offered to stay with me to keep me protected and even though I declined, he insisted I come here to stay so he can make sure that maniac doesn't get me. He's really a horrible person, so I can see your problem with him." She gets louder the longer she talks and I only hear a few sentences before I tune her out and just watch her lips move.

"When did you become this sexy?" That shuts her up and I instantly regret letting that come out of my mouth. I guess now that I've started this, I may as well continue and see what happens. I'm tired of fighting this attraction to her.

"Why are you doing this?" I move closer until I've pinned her against the kitchen cabinet. My body gravitates toward hers and it isn't until we're pressed together that I respond.

"Because I've waited too long to recognize what we have between us." She lowers her head, inhaling deeply against my chest. I can feel her heart beat faster the longer we stand together. Her internal struggle becomes too much for her when she pushes me away.

"Please don't. I can't take your bipolar reactions. It's not fair that you're doing this to me." I watch her walk up the stairs and into Levi's room before I adjust the bulging dick in my pants.

# Chapter Nine
## Kali

I rush up the stairs and fight back the tear in my eye as I take in what Noah just said. He's just as indecisive as he was years ago. He wants us and then he doesn't. Well, I can't take his shit right now. My life is a mess and the last thing I need is him burning what's left of my heart. I'm not sure I can walk away from another hit.

Levi is startled when I yank the door open to the bedroom and he's instantly looking at me with hungry eyes. "Come here, baby." He pats the bed beside him and rolls to his side. I can't do this. There's no way I can have sex with Levi after what I just went through downstairs. *I need to think.*

"I'm going for a run. I'll be back." Levi sits up quickly, throwing the covers off him.

"I'll come with you."

"No. That's okay." I try to reason with him, but I know it isn't going to work. I'm feeling suffocated and I'm about to explode.

"Kali. How many times do we have to go over this shit?"

"Fine. I'll come to bed with you, but please just give me some space. I need to think about some things and I can't do that if you're constantly wanting to have sex."

He stands, naked still from our swim last night. "Kali. I don't ever want you to feel like I'm pressuring you into sex. I'll give you space, just tell me what you need. Do you want me to stay in the guest bedroom?" And it takes that long for me to feel like the biggest bitch in the world. He's done nothing to deserve my claustrophobic reaction and I hate that I've done nothing but unload on him since last night.

"I'm sorry. It's just been a really shitty time lately and I'm trying to decide what my plan is. You're not staying in a guest bedroom, don't be ridiculous." I sit on my side of the bed and he follows my lead on his own side. We both lie back and he doesn't say a word while I try to get comfortable.

"Thank you for everything." I search for the

right words to make this better, but thank you is all I can come up with. I roll to my side and face away from him when Noah's words work their way back into my head. Levi wraps his arms around me and I can feel his breath against my neck.

"You're not alone in this. I'm here to help you through all of it, just tell me what's bothering you."

"I'm just trying to process all of this." He pulls me closer against him and I take a deep breath, acknowledging how great this feels. His dick twitches between us and I purposely ignore it and tuck my hand up next to my face as I curl into the covers a little tighter. Noah's cologne is on my hands and no matter how hard I fight to be right here with Levi in this moment, all my thoughts are with Noah.

*Damn him for this. He doesn't get to do this to me.*

I'm pissed off more than ever right now and the worst part is all of this is making me feel like I'm a weak bitch who can't deal with her own problems. Levi shouldn't have to save me. I need to save myself and these two men might be the first thing I need to run from.

Levi falls asleep and I roll over to face him, hoping he'll help me stop thinking about Noah. His stubble tickles my forehead, reminding me of our first night together. He's the first man I've ever been with that has facial hair. He's been amazing to me lately and I hate that I can't reciprocate all that he seems to be feeling. If things were different, I'd never let him go. I could get used to having this face with me every night, but I can't think like that when Noah is still circling my mind like he is.

There he is again, back in my thoughts. The more I think about everything the madder I get and before I know it, I can barely breathe with the heaviness of my frustration mixed with Levi's arms. I slide out from under his hold and decide I have to respond to Noah right now. Leaving this to fester in my mind will only be toxic for me and that's the last thing I need. I've lived with hope of having him in my life for too many years for him to play with my mind like this.

I walk through the house and find it empty. His bedroom door is open and I can hear the water running in his bathroom. Through the lump in my throat, I swallow hard and take the few steps it takes to get to the foot of his bed and sit quietly. Waiting for him to come out is a mind fuck, but I hold strong knowing I need to get this off my chest. He doesn't get to make me feel like this anymore.

He steps out, instantly seeing me. His hair is wet and his chest is covered with moisture. Steam rolls out of the bathroom behind him and for a moment I can't speak as I watch him approach me.

"You're not hiding this time." His voice snaps me back to reality, so I quickly stand. "If I would've known you'd be sneaking into my bedroom, I would've let *you* be the one to jack me off in the shower." His boldness surprises me, even though it shouldn't. He's obviously more secure with himself now than he ever was in high school. The Noah I knew never would've talked to me like he has the past few days.

"I'm only here to tell you that you have to stop. You don't get to play games with my head while you sit back and laugh at the destruction." He moves closer, slowly taking my breath away with every step he takes.

"Who says I'm playing games?"

"I do. You pushed me away just the other night if you don't remember, then I start seeing Levi and now you've conveniently changed your mind."

"I just came to my senses. You convinced me that I need to think about this a little *harder*." He takes my hand and puts it over the towel that's wrapped around his waist, pushing my hand into his own hardness as he says the word. I battle with the realization that I'm now the one playing games, pretending as if I haven't waited years for this and acting like I don't want it right now.

I pull my hand away, but he doesn't budge. He stands over me with every bit of confidence he's had since I walked into this house the other night.

"Tell me you haven't thought about what it'd be like to fuck me. To have my dick between your legs, making you scream until you don't have the energy to fucking walk." He pulls me against his body abruptly, lifting my chin until I'm looking into his eyes. "Can you tell me that, Kali?" I don't respond, because he'd know I'm lying if I told him I hadn't. And if I told him the truth, I'm afraid it would start something I'm not prepared to say no to.

"Stop." It's only a whisper, but it's enough to keep him from moving any closer. "Please just let me say what I came in here to say." He doesn't remove his hand from my neck or the one holding my lower back so that I'm pressed against him.

"Say what you came to say." *He's too close.* I thought I could feel the weight of him earlier, but that didn't compare to the heaviness I'm experiencing now. "Kali. Tell me that this isn't what you came for." He drops his towel and I push against his chest to get away from him.

"How can you do this to me?"

"Tell me what I'm doing." He walks over to the door, casually closing it before he turns to look at me again. He's naked and watching me differently than he has before. I'm almost afraid to know what he's thinking and what made him change the way he's acting towards me.

"I thought I was like family to you. That you can't be with me because of our parents being married and us living together fifteen damn years ago. Remember you telling me that you'll never be able to fuck me because you consider me a sister and that I'd only be a piece of ass to you." He looks down as I continue spouting off all the things he said to me the other night. "And now you think you can just drop your towel and what Noah? You think I'll just drop to my knees like a whore and take you to the back of my throat?"

I get louder the more I go on. I'm infuriated that he's shifting like this after I've started spending time with Levi. In fact, I'm actually enjoying what little time I've had with him where we weren't having some damn crisis of mine to deal with. "Why are you doing this now? After the way you've treated me the past few days and all the repulsed looks you've glared in my direction." He walks toward me as I walk backwards. I stop with my back against his door once again and he puts his palm on the door above my head just like he did the other night.

"I'm sorry, Kali. You don't repulse me. It's the opposite. Feel what you do to me." He pulls my right hand into his and moves it over his cock again. His lips move close to mine and I fight every ounce of restraint I have left to say one tiny word.

"No."

"Do you really mean no? Because if you say it one more time, I'm throwing you out of here." He stares into my eyes and even if I tried to pull away from him, I wouldn't get very far before I feel him again. He has this hold over me and he has almost my entire life. But I have to fight these feelings, even though I know I'll think about this moment countless times in the future.

I hate that I can't just stay in here and finally take what I've wanted for so long, but it all comes back to the way he treated me the other night. I can't and I won't put up with him being a complete asshole and he seems to be really good at it lately.

He pushes against me again, this time making sure his dick grinds against my pelvis. "Shit Kali, I've wanted to touch you for so long." His lips brush against mine just before he inhales deeply and slams his mouth over my lips. His tongue fights against my will power, taking away any chance I had of stopping this. Our hands grope with desperation and before I have a chance to realize what's happening, he's lifted my legs around his waist, sliding me higher on the door.

"I need you, Kali."

# Chapter Ten
## Noah

She's making me insane. Her kiss is every bit as tempting as I thought it'd be. Chaos filled with heavy breathing and desperation slams me straight into a frenzy of trying to get as close to her as I can.

Her hair drapes down between us, tangling in my fingers when I try to hold her head. It seems to cause her to freeze up and now she no longer matches the intensity coursing through my body.

I'm on fucking fire and she's going to pull away. I can feel her already doing it.

"I need you, Kali," I repeat and continue kissing her neck, biting just slightly when it's completely exposed for me.

"Noah, I can't." Her whisper against my ear should cause me to stop the trail of kisses I'm spreading over her chest, but it doesn't. Ignoring her should bring her back to where we were a few minutes ago, but it doesn't.

"Stop." She places her hand on my chest

again and I have no choice but to end what should be the first time we're having sex together.

"Can you tell me you're not craving this?" I grip her hair and force her to look into my eyes as my deep grumble comes out sounding just as frustrated as I am.

The raw emotion of being this close to her nearly has me setting her on her feet and walking away once again. There's so much between us and I know we haven't begun to scratch the surface of the issues we have, but right now in this moment all I can think of is sinking my dick deep inside her so I can listen to her moan for me this time.

"Not like this." Instant irritation spreads through me at her rejection. I let her slide down my body and take a few steps back. I start stroking my cock as I stand there looking at her. Her eyes drop immediately as she realizes what I'm doing.

"How then? On the bed, in the shower or we could always go for a fuck in the pool, since you seem to like that." Her stance shifts immediately, just like I knew it would. I know this is about to turn into a conversation about the past and what's festering between us. I'm not ready to talk about all of that; hell, it took everything in me just to approach her like I did just now.

"You're an ass for saying that."

"Well you did, seem to like it out there." My stroking slows, but I continue as she walks across the room.

"Can you stop doing that?" She's annoyed and for some reason that makes me happy, because there's no one in this house more infuriated than I am.

"Only if you take over. I'm not exactly a fan of having blue balls after you leave my bedroom again." She tilts her head as she processes what I'm saying.

"You didn't..."

"No, I didn't fuck those girls the other night. I kicked them out when I thought you left." For a brief minute, I see her trying to comprehend what's going on between us.

"Why did you treat me like that? I came here to check on you and wanted to see how your life is going." Sadness spreads over her face, making me feel guilty for causing her any more pain after the shitty few days she's been having.

"Because I wanted you to leave. I didn't want to think about what I'd do to you if given the chance." She sits on the edge of my bed and by now I've stopped jerking off and I'm trying to figure out how to move on from here. Do I treat her like shit to get her to leave and never come back to me, or do I slide her on her back and try to go after what I've been craving over half my life?

"You looked so cold that night. I've never seen you like that before." Her words are barely a whisper and her hair hides her face as she looks down at her fidgeting hands before she continues. "I've loved you my entire life and it dawned on me that night that I don't even know you. The Noah I know isn't capable of playing that dirty. You knew I was in here and you deliberately brought those girls in to rub in my face. That hurt."

"You snuck into my room." She interrupts me before I can say anything else.

"I didn't know it was your room. I just wanted to go somewhere private so I could wait on my ride without anyone seeing me like that." I move to sit next to her, not bothering to cover up with my towel or anything else for that matter.

"You liked watching, didn't you? I could feel you in the room. Wishing it was you there with me."

She doesn't respond, but her silence says everything. I slide my hand behind her neck, pulling her face toward me once again. She jerks away before I have the chance to kiss her. "We take turns fighting this, don't we, Kali?" She stands quickly, exhaling loudly before she starts pacing.

"I'm having fun with Levi. You don't get to play mind games with me. That's why I came in here in the first place." I watch her ass as it passes me a few times with her nervous striding back and forth.

"I'm not playing games. This is who I am, Kali. Still fucked in the head when it comes to you." She stops directly in front of me, focusing on my eyes and placing her hands on her hips. She looks sexy as fuck when she's mad. "I'd give anything to fuck that sass right out of you." I stand and stalk toward her slowly. She's about to give in, I can tell.

"How about we fuck first, talk later. Something tells me we'd have different things to talk about." I'm stroking myself again as I take the final few steps to reach her. Her eyes fall to my cock and I can't hold back the smirk that spreads across my face. "I've never had to work this hard for sex, but something tells me you're worth it."

"All these years I've wanted you to look at me like you are right this very minute. And now that you are, I can't stand it. I know you're only doing this because you don't want Levi to be with me." She walks to the door and this time I don't follow.

"You think you know me so well, Kali."

"I did know you. You've changed." She flips around to give me one last look before she reaches for the door knob.

"Maybe I have. But something tells me you like this guy." She slowly shakes her head, denying what I'm saying. "Why don't you stop playing the games now and drop to your knees?" Her jaw drops open when I say what I know she's itching to do. "Take my big cock to the back of that sexy throat until I control your breathing."

"Fuck you, Noah." She adjusts her clothes and yanks the door open, leaving in a haste. Levi walks by right after she walks out; the look on his face tells me he doesn't appreciate the fact that she just ran out of here while I stand here naked with my hand on my dick. Well, if it's any consolation, I'm not fond of it either.

"What the fuck did you just do?"

I pull a pair of sweats from the edge of the bed and slide them on before I answer. If he attacks me, I don't need my dick trying to help me kick his ass. "What I should've done years ago."

He walks in with his fucking hair standing on end in every direction, yet still looking like he could put on a suit and pull off a business look. "Did you fuck her?" He's pissed and he should be.

"Not yet." He charges at me, diving and slamming us both into my dresser.

"You fucking dick. You know she's staying with me." He lands a punch to my stomach and I get him in the jaw before Kali rushes in and starts screaming at both of us.

"Stop! Fucking stop it right now. I'm not dealing with this shit." She grips his shirt and pushes against my chest to separate us. "Levi, you don't get to fight over me. I'm not yours to fight over. And you ass," she shoves me and stands against me while she finishes. "I know you just antagonized him and I'm done playing your games. I'm getting a hotel until I can move back into my own house." She stomps out while we both work to catch our breath.

"Tell her I'm leaving on business and you both have the house for a week." Levi squints at me, knowing I'm lying about having a business trip, but he doesn't argue with me or try to ask questions. We both know it'll be easier this way.

I start folding some clothes into a suitcase while he stands there and watches me. "Did your ass really finally decide to give in to her?"

His words make me pause as I think of the best way to respond to him. "Yes."

"What is it you want from her?"

"I don't want anything. It was a stupid move on my part and it's obvious we'll never be anything more than whatever the fuck we are right now." He doesn't respond. He just watches me with curiosity in his face. I need to avoid talking to him too, since he's made it his life mission recently to tell me how I've fucked up for years where Kali is concerned. I don't need another reminder; there's enough torture in my own thoughts about her already.

# Chapter Eleven
## Kali

It's been four days since Noah left and that's how long I've been trying to process everything he said to me before he walked out the door. Levi has been extremely helpful and has even given me the space I've needed to think about things, but I can feel him trying to pull away. I refuse to let him. He's been an amazing friend to me over the past week and I don't know how I would've made it without him.

"What are your plans for the day?" Levi rolls toward me, rubbing his face in the process.

"I'm going to take your friend up on that offer and take that job at Mike's. I need normalcy in my life." He sits up quickly before he leans over me.

"You're going to get so fucking tired of seeing me. But at least this way I can make sure you're safe." He's taking a few shifts as a bouncer at one of his friend's clubs. I'll be waitressing because Mike assured me I'd make great tips, so I'm sure this will help me get some money saved up fast to get a car again.

"I doubt I'll get tired of you. I just want to get some money saved up so I can get a new place and a car."

"You can take my truck until you buy a car. I can ride the bike until then." He has a motorcycle that I haven't seen him on yet.

"What would I do without you?"

"You'd be lost." He leans over to leave a peck on my lips before he climbs over me and walks into the bathroom, closing the door. There's that pulling away I've been feeling.

I throw the covers off my legs and follow him, opening the door to him standing in front of the toilet taking a piss.

"You want to hold it for me or something?" He turns just enough that I can see his dick and the stream of pee flowing from it.

"No. Why are you pulling away from me?" He lowers his head again, turning so I can't see his face.

"I'm giving you the space you need to figure out your life. Believe me, it's not something

I want to do." He shakes off the last few drips before he turns the shower on.

"Then stop. If I'm going to figure this out, I need you to be normal with me. I don't want you to hold back because I'm not some fragile woman that can't handle you at your best." He smiles and exhales in relief.

"Thank god. My dick is going to fall off if I don't get to touch you soon." He approaches me with a hunger in his eyes and I don't make him say anything more before I start pulling my tank top and shorts off.

"Jesus, Kali. How did you get to be so perfect?" His breath hits my ear, sending chills over my naked skin.

"You're not so bad yourself, you know. A girl could get used to waking up next to this face every morning." I grip his chin in my hand and pull his face toward mine. He doesn't give me a chance to say anything further before he covers my lips with his. He pulls the shirt off his back and kicks his shorts off in record time.

Grabbing my ass, he lifts me around his

waist. The muscles in his arms shift under my hands and I take this opportunity to explore him all over again. As my fingers run down his back, he moves us until my back is against the wall in the shower and the water is racing down both of our bodies.

He moves fast to position himself, making the first thrust inside me exquisite. He's everything I've always wanted in a man, yet my mind haunts me even in this very moment. He's not Noah.

He never will be. So why does he feel so right and Noah seems like everything I should steer clear of?

"Kali, you're tight as fuck. Are you clenching down on my dick?" I realize my mind has me tense when I need to be focused on Levi. Releasing my muscles allows him to thrust deep this time. "Ah fuck. That's it. Let me in." He grips my hair, pulling my head back before he moans into my neck.

He claws and grips my body while he fucks me against the wall. I feel him everywhere and with that he makes me forget about Noah. He consumes me and takes me places I've never been when my body begins to shiver and explode into an orgasm so strong that I have no choice but to scream in pain and pleasure at the same time.

He doesn't stop thrusting even when I become so sensitive that I'm trying to pull away from him. His moaning becomes like a growl when he reaches his own orgasm as he pulls out and sends his cum all over the shower wall beside us. "Fuck, you make me crazy. I needed that this morning." He runs his hand through his crazy hair, allowing the water to tame the mess on top of his head.

"You don't exactly make me calm." He smiles an ornery grin before he hits me back with his banter.

"Maybe I like you crazy." This is how we are. He's fun and always playful. He's exactly what I need in my life. He's not out to fuck with my mind or cause me to feel inadequate about my shortcomings. Levi has always made me feel like I deserve to be happy. Even when he tried to get me to forget about Noah and move on with my life, his intentions were to make me realize that I need to respect myself enough to know Noah doesn't dictate my happiness.

"Maybe I like *you* crazy."

"Nah, you love my crazy. You think it's sexy." He's right. I'm beginning to love his crazy and I sure as hell think it's sexy.

# Chapter Twelve
## Kali

"Look at that ass." Levi steps close behind me, pulling me against his hips as I'm bent over wiping a table clean.

"Stop. I told you to keep it professional at the club. I don't need you distracting me." He releases me with a giant grin on his face.

"Always so serious. I love that I know the relaxed Kali."

"Away from here you can be like that, but when I'm at work I need you to respect that I'm busy."

"Oh I know. I just couldn't resist that ass of yours."

"Well, thank you. I think." I grab the tray of empty glasses and turn to look at him. "I get off in an hour. What time will you be done?"

"I'm here till midnight. Are you going to hang around here or head to the house?" He shifts into his serious protective Levi.

"I'll head to your house and take a shower. I'll be there when you get home and maybe we can start where we left off this morning." His eyes light up and I can't help but match his smile. He makes me feel amazing and I want to spend time with him.

"How do you feel about going for a run in the morning before work? Or maybe some grocery shopping?"

"I'm in. We also should go check out some houses. I told Noah I'd find a place to stay soon. You can stay with me until you get your place. Or if you decide to never leave, I'd be fine with that too." His smile says everything and in this moment, I don't see anything wrong with seeing where this relationship goes.

"Sounds like a plan. Let's see how everything goes. I'll see you later tonight." I take the last tray to the kitchen and clock out. Mike already told me how great I was doing and said I could leave once the last table was cleared.

Levi follows me out to his truck, just like I thought he would. He also kisses me as hard as I hoped he would. "Now see, out here it's okay. In fact, I want you to grope me and act like you can't keep your hands off me."

"I think I can handle that." He pulls me against his chest for a hug just before some commotion disturbs us back at the club entrance. "Looks like I need to help at the door. I'll see you in a couple of hours."

He doesn't leave me until I'm in the truck so he can close the door. Levi has a way of making me feel safe and I love that about him. It's something I never knew I was missing until he showed me what it feels like.

I look down at the clock on my drive home and realize it's been exactly a week from right now that I was at Levi's house for the party, seeing Noah for the first time in years. My nerves were all over the place, but I'm glad I took the chance and went. The curiosity was killing me. It's amazing how everything can change in just a few days.

I park as close to the house as I can and rush inside once I get there. I guess that has become a habit lately with the asshole neighbor living next door.

Once the door is locked again, I take a deep breath and flip on a few lights. The house is quiet, so I hit the remote, sending music through the speakers and begin to move freely around the house. I've done everything I can to make sure nothing is out of place in Noah's house. I don't need him to have any reasons to get pissed when he returns.

My plan is to be out of here by then, but something tells me he'd hold a grudge for years if I do anything even in the slightest to irritate him.

I'm wiping down the bar when I hear the front door slam. I rush to see who it is only to come face to face with Noah in the living room. "Don't mind me. Please continue to move around the house in that slutty little outfit of yours. I happen to like watching you."

"You were watching me? What the hell, Noah?" I move to check all the curtains before he has a chance to respond.

"Sue me." He starts up the stairs without another word and my heart beats so hard I can feel throughout my body.

Why does he still have the power to do this to me? He's an asshole.

# Chapter Thirteen
## Noah

Those fucking shorts should be outlawed in public. Her ass cheeks are out to tease the world and torture me to fucking death. I take the stairs two at a time and don't hear any noise behind me, not that I'd stop from stripping if she did follow.

I've been driving for four days trying to figure out what I'm doing with my life, only to return with a more chaotic mind than when I left. Kali is my weakness; she always has been. The one thing I did figure out on my soul-searching trip is that I regret not giving in to her sooner. It's always been Kali. I've dated women for years and every single one of them had to endure my critical comparison to Kali. And every single one of them came up short.

I hear Levi's bedroom door close just before I start taking a piss. She's hiding from me. I don't blame her. But sadly, that door being closed isn't going to stop what I'm about to say to her.

Pulling the old photo album from the top of my closet and a new t-shirt from a hanger, I leave my room on a mission to talk to her. I give her the courtesy of a knock before I open the door. She's surprised.

"I didn't say you could come in."

"Yeah, you see; it's my house so I don't have to be invited." I feel like a dick for saying that, but it's what slips out before I have the chance to stop it.

"What do you want, Noah?" She's irritated with me.

"Thought you should see something. We can either do this in here or you can meet me back downstairs." She scans the bed before she responds.

"Downstairs." I let my eyes move over the bed and then back to the uncomfortable look on her face before I turn around and leave the room. She fucks Levi in that bed, of course she doesn't feel relaxed having me in that room.

I'm in the kitchen pouring myself a drink when she makes an appearance. She's now wearing sweatpants and a baggy t-shirt, I'm sure in an attempt to keep me from making any moves on her. Little does she know there's not a thing she could put on that would cause me to not be attracted to her.

I open the photo album and turn my back to it as she sits down at the bar. "This is why I've struggled with what we have between us. Do you see what your mom made me after my father left her?" I listen to her turn page after page of the scrapbook that has haunted me for years.

Glancing over my shoulder, I see that she's engrossed with each page. "Noah, I had no idea my mom sent you this."

"She sent a new section every year. I added to that book until she stopped sending me pages."

"Jesus. No wonder you've fought this. She put the word sister on every page."

"I know she did." She looks up from the album before she gets to the end.

"We aren't blood related Noah. What I've felt for you all these years goes deeper than that.

I've loved you by choice, not by some fate of nature that we're related and I'm forced into respecting you. I loved you because you understood me. You made me feel like I belonged somewhere." Tears fill her eyes and it takes everything in me not to go around the bar and dry them like I have in the past.

"I've always loved you. But it was never enough for you." I drink my whiskey and watch her finish the album while she fights the tears threatening to slide down her face. "Thank you for showing me this." And before I can speak around the lump in my throat, she's walked out of the room and is running up the stairs.

I pour myself another glass and contemplate how I'm supposed to react to her. No matter how many times I've tried to deny what I've felt over the years, she's always there lingering in the background torturing my mind. I throw the last swig of my drink back and decide to go for what's mine.

This time I take the stairs one at a time, playing in my head exactly what I'm going to say when I open her door. I should feel guilty coming at her like I have been now that she's playing around with Levi, but we all know that isn't real.

Standing next to the closed door, I can hear water running. She's in the shower; I can't think of a better time to tell her how I feel. She failed to lock the door. That's something she'll learn to do if she wants to keep me out.

I can see her naked silhouette behind the rough glass door. Her head is tilted back while she lets the water soak into her long hair. Her tits move just slightly as she runs her fingers through her hair. I could watch her like this all day, but I'm not going to miss this opportunity. Kicking my shoes off, I slide the door open and step in. It takes her a second to see me and just like I thought she'd do, she screams before she tries to cover herself.

I pull her hands into mine to calm her. "Stop. I'm just here to talk." Her breathing is heavy and her eyes search me, trying to understand what I'm doing. I brush the hair off her cheek and lick my lips before I say one word.

The water continues to drench my shirt and jeans.

"I've always loved you too." The lump in my throat seems to be growing the more I talk. "You've been more than enough for me. But the truth is, I'm afraid I'll ruin you." I rub my thumb over her lower lip when she starts to say something. "Kali, it's what I do. You deserve better than me, yet here I am fighting against everything I've told myself for years."

"Noah," she whispers against my fingers. Her grip on my jeans tightens and for a second I imagine ripping my clothes off and fucking her right here in Levi's shower. Her face is tormented as she fights whatever is fucking with her mind and I know I need to leave this shower. I may be a giant dick, but this is even beyond my capabilities.

"Take your time finding a place. You can stay here as long as you need to. I'll keep my distance, unless you come to me for more." She doesn't release her grip on me even when I drop my hands to my sides. She grips tighter, pulling me toward her.

I slide a hand behind her neck and pull her face toward mine. My kiss is soft and gentle. I know if I let this go any further, she'll hate herself for doing anything while she's still connected to Levi. I need to let her have time to figure things out for herself. If she decides she wants him, I'll have to learn to live with it, but at least now she knows how I feel.

I step out of the shower and pull a towel from the rack. I even pull off my jeans so I don't track footsteps through the house. If Levi sees my wet tracks trailing through his room, he's liable to kill me in my sleep. If the tables were turned, that's exactly what I'd do.

# Chapter Fourteen
## Levi

I see Noah's truck in the driveway when I pull up to the house and my mind instantly goes into a panic wondering what he's said to Kali. He hasn't been exactly welcoming to her, so I hope he hasn't said anything tonight to contradict me telling her she's welcome to stay with us.

The house is quiet when I step inside until I hear a glass being set down in the kitchen. When I turn the corner, Noah is standing behind the bar, pouring two glasses of whiskey. "Have a drink with me."

"What's the occasion?" I drop my stuff on the table and take a stool at the bar, watching him closely as I try to figure out where his head is.

"Do I need a special occasion to drink with my best friend of fifteen years?"

"Thought you were going to be gone for a week." He hands me one of the glasses and leans back against the cabinet, facing me while he slowly sips the whiskey from the glass.

"I drove for four days, then decided I was ready to be home." I follow his lead and sip the drink, eyeing him over the rim.

"Four days of driving. It's been a while since you've pulled that stunt." I know him. He only drives like that when it involves Kali. He uses the road as his thinking time, only in the past it was for two days at a time.

"Yeah, I guess it has." His voice becomes lower when I hear footsteps behind me. I don't look back to see Kali, I know it's her by the look on his face.

She sits next to me, not saying a word while she watches Noah turn and pull out a bottle of tequila. "I think it's time we all have a shot together." His eyes lock on hers while he pours the first shot, then he doesn't make eye contact with her again. I can tell he's up to something and I'm half tempted to beat his ass just for what my mind is concocting as a possible scenario of his intentions.

"To fucking off in the past, fucking for fun in the present, and fucking up in the future." He lifts his shot glass and holds it over the bar as he waits for us to both join him. I raise mine and she slowly follows, both of us looking at him like he's a mental case ready to blow.

"That's a lot of fucking, my dear friend."

"You should relate to that," he shoots back quickly, pouring us all another shot.

"Noah, what are you doing?" Her voice is low, almost like she's scared to poke the crazy that's lingering in the room.

"Can't a guy just have a few drinks with his friends?" He hands her the shot glass again, both glaring imaginary daggers into each other's eyes before she takes it.

"One more and I'm going to go shower the trashy whores off me," I speak up, interrupting their intense zoned in behavior. There's obviously something going on between these two and even though I'm finding myself falling for Kali, I won't be a barbarian and push her to feel the same for me when I know how she's felt about Noah her entire life. She has to fall for me because I'm the better option, not out of guilt.

"Kali, why don't you do the honors this time? What are we toasting to?" Noah puts her on the spot and I watch her shift in her seat while she thinks about a toast. My eyes fall to her long braided hair, still damp from her shower.

"To taking it one day at a time." I watch him smirk and lift his glass, so I follow. This one didn't taste as smooth as the other one, but it might be me choking on the thoughts swirling around in my head.

"I'm headed up to shower." She turns toward me and surprises me with a soft kiss. I let my tongue slide over hers a few times before I pull back and look her in the eyes. "I'll be back down in a few." Her smile allows me to leave her with a confidence that she's still feeling me, even though I'm not pushing.

"Sounds great." She gives me one last kiss before I leave the two of them alone. I decide I need to hurry my ass up and show back up as the usual Levi and leave this tired asshole upstairs.

# *Kali*

Noah is playing games even though he said he'd leave me alone unless I approached him. I can tell Levi caught on to his shenanigans and I know I'll need to tell him everything soon. He deserves the truth from me and I can only hope he doesn't hate me for what has happened the past few days.

"Was that little show for me?" Noah's irritation is obvious by the sound of his voice.

"It wasn't a show, Noah. You know I've been spending time with Levi lately. He's actually really nice to me."

"Oh, I don't doubt that."

"Don't be like that. You have to give me time to process all of this." I stand with the intention of going upstairs to escape his rude demeanor when he moves around the bar to meet me.

"Tell me. Do you think he could still taste my kiss on these sexy lips of yours?" He rubs his thumb over my bottom lip, wiping away any moisture Levi left behind.

"What makes you think I didn't scrub my lips once you left?" He squints his eyes before he responds with a mischievous grin on his face.

"Because we both know you slid two fingers in that pussy of yours and thought of me while you were left wanting the real thing."

"Is this you keeping your distance? Because to me it feels like you're coming at me from all angles." He puts his hand down at his side and allows his eyes to brush over my face. I can almost feel him as he takes all my features in.

"You're fucking gorgeous and you have no idea. That alone makes you dangerous." I don't respond to him; that's what he wants from me. He's making it very clear that he won't be giving me my space to figure things out. He's going to be very aggressively torturing me until I either give in to him or leave so he can't get to me.

Levi has been amazing to me and I can't shake how I'm beginning to feel about him, but at what point do I try to process how I've felt for years and try to compare that to what I've been experiencing with Levi the past week or so?

"Drink with me. Maybe when Levi comes down we can all get to know each other a little better. Since we've missed out on so much of each other's lives." He leaves me standing by myself on this side of the bar while he pours another drink for both of us.

"Is your plan to get me drunk?"

"And what if it is? Truth tends to come out when someone has liquid courage." He watches me closely as he reaches over the bar once again, handing me my glass. "Something tells me you'll react differently after another one of these." I wonder if Noah is only acting like this because he's mad at Levi for what we've been doing and this is his way at revenge.

Maybe he hopes I'll give in and then he can rub it in Levi's face while he throws me out to the world alone once again because he can't handle our connection. Who knows what he's up to, but I can handle a few drinks and remain clear headed. He has no idea what I've been doing with my life if he thinks two drinks will have me spilling all my secrets.

The only thing I know is I can't lose Levi right now. He makes me feel secure and safe and that's something I haven't had in my life. It's something I'm not willing to lose.

"I'm not one of your light weight floozies, Noah. I can hold my own. You pressuring me into drinking won't change my dilemma." I won't go into how much I'm starting to care about Levi; he won't believe me anyway. With Noah, everything is about him so he won't understand how I'm feeling, even if I try to explain it to him.

"I'm hearing a challenge!" Levi yells out from the stairs before he enters the kitchen to join us again.

"That's what I've been saying." Noah looks to Levi as if he'll help encourage me to drink.

"Maybe we should hit the golf course for a little round of glow in the dark, like the old days." Noah smiles the second the words come out of Levi's mouth.

"Have fun, boys. This girl still doesn't play

golf."

"I'll teach you." Levi towel dries his messy hair while his blue eyes work to convince me to do anything he says.

"Yeah, he can teach you." Noah throws back another shot before he walks out of the room. "I'll call Mike and tell him we'll be on the green so he doesn't send the cops out to get us like the old days."

"Is he harassing you?"

"I can handle Noah." Levi moves close enough that his scent hits me just before he pops the towel toward my leg.

"Never said you couldn't." He turns to face me as I rush to stand and retaliate with the hand towel from the bar.

"Not the dick. Not the dick." He stutters and stands solid with his hands covering him, but allowing me to hit him in the leg before he grabs me in a bear hug, swinging me around the room a few times.

"You're insane."

"You just realizing this?" He stops spinning

us, pulling me against his bare chest and allowing me to inhale his sexy scent all over again while he kisses me. His hands begin to grope me and all I can think about is the chance of Noah coming in to see this and what he'd say.

"You should go with Noah. I think it would be good for the two of you to spend some time together." He grips both of my arms and pulls me away from his chest.

"Not a chance. I only agreed to do this because I want to spend more time with you. If you want to ditch, I'd be more than happy to spend time with you in my bedroom."

"Levi, I feel bad doing all of this in Noah's house. Maybe I should try to get a hotel or something for a week."

"If that's what you want, we can go tomorrow. But I'm not letting you go by yourself until I can get the guys to get that neighbor of yours taken care of. I have a friend working on a few things." I don't ask questions when he turns his back toward me. Something tells me I don't want to know what they're up to, but I won't feel bad if they do *handle* him.

"Thank you, Levi." My soft voice has him looking over his shoulder mid-step before he leaves me standing in the kitchen alone.

"You're welcome, Kali."

# Chapter Fifteen
## Noah

If I have to watch him wrap his arms around her again, I may drive this fucking golf cart straight into the water.

"Line it up and just tap it. You've got this one." I try to encourage from the cart, hoping to give his overly attentive ass a break from grinding up against her on this shot.

She glares over at me. I know she can tell I'm irritated. Hell, Levi must know too, unless he's just an idiot. My guess is he doesn't give a shit and actually enjoys seeing me raging like a lunatic.

"All right, you drink again, Kali." She's starting to slur her words and has quickly moved into the no go zone for what I was hoping to accomplish tonight.

She was supposed to get tipsy and then I'd get her to start talking and she'd tell us how she truly feels. I'm ready to get Levi out of the picture when it comes to Kali. She's mine and she always has been and that's something he has known for years.

"I'm done. I can't hit that little ball when I'm sober. I'll be drinking at every hole if we keep this up."

"If you want me to drink for you on the rest of the holes, I will. Just remember you have to deal with the whiskey dick when we get back." It takes everything inside me not to run him over as I watch him slap her on the ass and I have to hear her laugh. Fuck all of this. I never should've came out here with them tonight. Levi isn't going to step aside easily on this, he's making that very clear with every moment that passes.

It's the eighteenth hole and Levi is a blubbering drunk. She seems to be sobering up some, but at this point I've joined in just to dull the sharpness of the banter between the two of them.

"Fuck, I'm drinking again." Levi lies in the grass after his last shot. He knows he's done for. "Noah, I'm watching you." I hear his comment, but ignore it as I help him up.

"Come on. I'll get us back to the house." My house sits near the golf course and Mike won't mind if I borrow the cart till morning. I can go through the field this way and stay off the roads.

I sit him on the back seat while she slides in next to where I'll be sitting. "This was fun." The moon lights up her face, allowing me to see her smile. For a brief second I'm frozen, just taking everything about her in.

"Noah, what are you doing?" I watch her lips say my name and fight like hell to keep from kissing her. I wage war on myself for the thoughts going through my head and wish I could be the guy that takes what he wants and doesn't give a shit about the consequences. I know if I do anything tonight, she'll never forgive me and that's not something I'm ready to deal with again.

"Taking you home." She doesn't say a word on the way back to the house. I drive in silence and try to sort the chaos going on in my mind. She's the woman I've always loved and

I've lost her because I've been afraid my entire life of what other people would think. I've been miserable making other people happy.

I park the cart in my parking spot and she staggers into the house, leaving Levi for me to take in. I'm half dragging him to the couch when I hear her throwing up in the back bathroom.

"Kali, are you okay in there?"

"Go away, Noah." She's hurling before she finishes saying my name. I open the door to her hugging the toilet, her hair hanging all around her face.

"Fuck. I'm not good at this shit Kali." I pull her hair back and wait for her to finish throwing up before I toss her a towel and help her up. "I'm going to put you in the guest bedroom down here tonight. He's passed out on the couch already." She nods, agreeing with me while I help her out of the bathroom and across the hall.

"I'm sorry I'm such a pain, Noah. I don't want to be." Her words ring in my ears and it hits me that she has no idea that I've always wanted her and the issues she brings into my life. I have to talk to her again, but tonight is not the time.

I help her under the covers and before I have the chance to leave the room she surprises me with a whisper, "Stay with me, Noah."

"Kali, I can't."

"Please." I stand over her as she dozes off and then opens her eyes again, searching for me. "Noah. Please." Even though this isn't how I pictured the two of us in bed together for the first time, I slide in beside her. She moves against me and I hold her against me. Both of us fully clothed and at least one of us having a heart slamming moment, realizing what's been missing in life.

# Chapter Sixteen
## Kali

I wake up wrapped in Noah's arms, feeling more guilt than I thought possible. What have I done? My thoughts try to wrap around the possibility that Levi saw us and what I'd say to him.

Sliding out of bed slowly is easier than staying quiet while I gather my things. I have to get out of this house. I'm suffocating myself with these two men and I don't know how to allow myself a chance to breathe.

I open the front door with my bags draped over my shoulders knowing I can't come back here again. It's best for all of us. The way I'm handling things right now isn't healthy for me or either of them for that matter.

The neighborhood is quiet so it's easy to hear the door open behind me. It's a fifty-fifty guess as to who it is, but I don't turn around to look. I can't face either of them right now.

"Kali." Noah's deep grumble slides over my skin like it always does.

"Noah, don't try to stop me. Tell Levi I'll return his truck as soon as I can get a loaner."

"Tell him yourself. I'm not wasting possibly my last few seconds with you talking about him or his things." I face the door to the truck; it's better if I don't look at him. He's already tormenting me enough. Whatever he's about to say will only make what I'm going through worse.

He holds the door closed with his palm over my head like he always seems to do. "We need to talk."

"We've said enough. I need to think and I can't do that with the two of you suffocating me."

"Where will you be?" His voice is louder this time as he leans closer.

"I'm not sure yet. I'll text you both and let you know." He slides his hand down my side, forcing my eyes closed while I take in what he's doing to me.

"How will I know you're safe?" He drops his hands to his side and takes a step back.

"I'm not your worry, Noah. I can handle myself." I open the door and throw the last bag into the seat before I turn around.

"I never said you couldn't, but that won't stop me from worrying about you being safe from that psychotic neighbor of yours."

"Thank you for allowing me to stay at your house." Before he has a chance to stop me or say anything to make me change my mind, I slide in and close the door. He watches me leave and I make myself stop looking in the rear-view mirror as I pull away, hoping I don't regret this one day.

# Noah

She's out of her fucking mind if she thinks I'm just going to let her leave without saying what I need to say. I turn to follow her only to find my truck is still at the golf course, leaving me with only this cart to chase her down with.

Call me crazy, but I'm not thinking that would be the best way to make my point and win her over.

I drive the cart back to Mike and get my truck before I go back to the house to take a shower. The water washes over me and all I can think of is how she felt against me in bed last night. How her smile and the sound of her laughter made the entire night perfect.

I'm pulling a shirt over my head when Levi passes my doorway. "Where's Kali?"

"She's gone."

"What do you mean she's gone? What the fuck did you do?" His first thought is to blame me, just like it should be.

"She said she needed space and she'd return your truck as soon as she could." He's pulling out his phone before I can say anything further and I don't stop him. If he can convince her to come back, then that'll make it easier on me to have the chance to talk to her.

# Levi

I get her voicemail. I feel like dog shit because I drank so much last night. This hangover isn't helping me think about what I'm going to say when she answers, but it doesn't stop me from obsessively calling her over and over again.

On the seventh call she answers, "Levi. Please."

"Please what? Let you get raped by that fucking dick neighbor of yours, not a chance sweetheart. Get your ass back to this house before I fire up my bike to come find you."

"I need space. You two are smothering me to death and I need to think."

"What's there to think about? The only thing you need to be worried about right now is your damn safety. Where are you going?" I fire back sounding more irritated than I mean to. This fucking hangover isn't helping this conversation go as smoothly as it should be.

"I was just going to drive until I found a place to stop. Thought maybe the open road could allow me some time to process everything." I can feel her pulling away from me. It has to be Noah.

"I'll go with you."

"Levi. You're one of the reasons I need to think and I can't do that with you around me."

"I get that. Just come back here and I'll

give you all the space you need. You can stay in the guest bedroom and I won't bother you as long as I know you're safe." My overwhelming instinct to protect her is on overdrive right now, no thanks to what my buddies found out about the neighbor. "Look, you can't under any circumstances go to your house alone. I need you to promise me you're coming back here and I'll give you what you need. Just do this for me so I don't go back to jail making sure you're safe from that fucker again." I'm pulling off my clothes as I wait for her response. One way or another I have to get to her and I'm not going to waste time if she tries to make me work for this.

"All right. I'll come back, but we need to talk as soon as I get there." She sounds defeated and sad. It kills me to hear her struggling like she is and there's nothing I wouldn't do to fix that for her.

"I'll get in the shower now. Text me when you're here and I'll come out to the truck." She disconnects the call and I rush to take my shower. If I didn't feel so much like ass, I'd have skipped it, but it seems to help immensely.

I make a mad dash to the kitchen and throw together a sandwich and grab a Gatorade, managing to get it down before she texts that she's here. Noah hasn't made another appearance by the time I head out the door to see her.

She looks like hell and I get in slowly as I try to ease into whatever conversation she wants to have. "Thank you for making it easy on me. You know I would've driven this entire town looking for you if that's what it took."

"Levi, you don't have to protect me."

"I know that, but I want to. That guy is bad fucking news and until he's out of the picture I still want to keep an eye on you. Now, what has you running from my house this morning?" She looks down at the steering wheel instantly.

"I need time to think, like I said."

"I'll give you that. I'll give you whatever you want, just come back inside and I'll let you come to me when you're ready to talk." Her eyes are filled with tears when she looks up at me.

"Levi, I've loved Noah for so many years that I don't know anything different and now you've somehow creeped through the cracks of my broken heart." She pauses and swallows hard before she continues. "And now he's decided to give in to the supposed feelings he has as well, but I've refused him." I knew this conversation was coming when she left the house in such a hurry this morning. "I refused him because of how I feel about you." I turn to her with hope, but it's only heartbreak that's spread across her face. She's truly torn about this and that makes me realize what I must do.

I have to leave her alone so she can decide what she wants. She's held onto the slight chance that Noah would reciprocate her feelings for years now and I can't be the reason she doesn't give herself a chance with him. I don't want her regretting anything if she's with me and if that means I step back and give her the space she needs, then that's what I'll do.

We both sit quietly until I finally respond. "I care about you, Kali. And because of that, I want you to see if there's anything between you and Noah. I've watched the two of you over the years fight the temptations and if you're both finally on the same page... I could never hold you back from that." I speak past the lump in my throat and give her what she needs to move forward.

"Levi, I don't know what I feel. I'm literally all over the place and it's making me insane."

"Who says you have to make a decision today? Stay with us at the house and take time until you decide what you want." It'll suck if I have to say goodbye to her and out of the slim chance that she'll realize what we have is the beginning of greatness, I'm pushing to have her stay.

I want Kali in my life. She makes me smile and everything is fun with her. She's always been different than any other woman, I just didn't realize how much different she'd be when I really got to know her and how much I'd love that difference.

"I don't want to hurt you." She won't look at me this time, so I reach across the truck and lift her chin until she has no choice.

"Look at me." I stop a tear from trailing down her cheek. "You won't hurt me. I want you happy and if that means you're with Noah, then that's what I want." I don't tell her that it'll gut me; she doesn't need that bit of information weighing on her mind.

"Now come inside and I'll help you get your stuff set up in the spare room." We both open our doors at the same time and then I let her follow me inside. Noah is in the kitchen when we pass, but neither of us stop to fill him in. I need to have a little one on one talk with him about all of this anyway.

"You know where to find me if you need anything."

"Thank you, Levi. Here are your keys." She attempts to hand my truck keys back to me and I don't reach for them.

"I told you to keep it until you found something to replace your Jeep."

"I know you did, but I can't keep getting handouts from you."

"It's not a handout; you're just borrowing it

until you get yours." I walk toward the door, knowing she's not going to make it easy to reason with her about this. "I have to work tonight at the club; will I see you there for your shift?"

"Yes. I'll be there." It makes me oddly at ease knowing I'll get to see her tonight. I walk out, leaving her to think and giving myself a chance to see what Noah has been up to.

# Chapter Seventeen
## Noah

"We need to fucking talk." Levi slams his hand on the patio table, rattling my coffee cup and everything else in the process.

"What's your problem?" The sun shines around his body, so I can't see his expression, but I know this is about Kali. Levi doesn't generally let anything bother him. I guess that's changed now.

"My problem is your ass needs to figure out what you're doing. The rest of the world isn't going to sit back and wait while you decide when you'll allow Kali into your life or not. I'm fucking done seeing her hurt, so if that's what you have as a grand plan, change it now." He sits in the chair opposite me and glares with an anger I'm not used to seeing in him.

"Who says I haven't figured it out?"

"We'll see. But just know I'll kick your ass if you lead her on only to throw her out again." He cares about her. It's written all over his face.

"Holy shit. You're not just playing around

with her, are you? You're falling for Kali." He stands abruptly, not looking at me again as he walks toward the sliding door.

"All you need to know is if you fuck up, I'll be there ready to sweep in and save her while I kick your ass." He leaves me sitting by myself outside and I wonder what she said to him exactly.

It seems like she broke it off with him to see what could come between us. I take the last sip of my coffee and slide inside, hoping to see her again. This couldn't have worked out better for me this morning.

# Kali

I'm still staring at the door to my new room when I hear a quick knock and see Noah peek in. "So you decided to stay." He opens the door, proudly walking in with his head held high like he just won a competition.

"For a few days."

"Good. It'll give us time." He sits on the edge of my bed and falls back, watching me as I move around the room.

"No, it'll give me time. Just like I told Levi, I need to do some soul searching and you two are the reason I left in such a hurry this morning. I can't breathe while you give me whiplash and Levi does everything I've ever wanted."

"You can't be serious about Levi." I turn quickly, flashing him a stern look that shuts him up quickly.

"He's been amazing and I won't let you talk shit about him." He sits up, raising his hands in defeat.

"Fine. He's a great guy. Now let's talk about me." He's so damn conceited that I want to choke him. How do I let him get to me like he does?

"You're an ass. You've made that very clear over the years and you haven't pulled back the past week either." He stands and stalks toward me, slowly watching me take a step back with each one he takes forward.

"Just remember, you came to me. You've creeped into my bedroom more than once now, so don't get pissed at me for this little predicament." His breath hits my cheek as he finishes his sentence. His mouth is dangerously close to mine as he continues. "And now look where we are. Back to where we were the first night in my bedroom with your back against the wall and your eyes begging me to rip your clothes off so I can fuck you."

"My eyes aren't begging for anything." I step around him, leaving him standing by the door alone.

"You forget that I've known you most of your life."

"You forget that you haven't been around me the last few years and you don't know me like you used to." He rubs his chin and leans against the door frame, imitating someone pondering one of life's great mysteries.

"You're right. It looks like I'll need to change that in the next few days. Get a shower and change. I'm taking you somewhere." He swings the door open quickly and leaves like a man on a mission.

"I have to work tonight."

"I'll have you there in time. No excuses Kali, get ready." His voice gets further away before he finishes.

He has no boundaries. He's established that many times, but the way he's ordering me to get dressed on command, reminds me of the old Noah. The one that I fell for years ago.

~~~~~~

"Get in. I'm taking you to one of my favorite thinking places. Something tells me you'll find it just as relaxing as I do." He has the passenger window down when I step outside.

I glance over and see that Levi's motorcycle is gone. I thought I heard the rumble of the engine just before Noah stepped into my room.

"How far are we going?"

"It's just a few miles."

We both sit in silence as the trees pass

while he takes me down the road and into a wooded area that I didn't even know you could go back into. The small road isn't meant to be traveled and the further we go, the more I can tell this place will feel remote and give me the peace and serenity I need.

The view is gorgeous when we finally park in front of a small waterfall. I don't wait for him to say anything before I'm out of his truck, walking toward the water.

I've always been drawn to water and that's something he knows. "I love it." Taking in everything in sight, I keep walking until I'm at the edge. He follows me and sits on a large rock. He hits the empty space next to him a couple of times to get me to sit with him.

"This place is gorgeous. And so quiet. You were right about me liking it."

"See, I remember the important things about you." I can feel him looking at me while I continue to take in our surroundings. "I even remember the expressions you make when you're happy." I lower my head at his words. Just when I think he's still the giant ass he's always been, he does something like this and surprises me.

"Why are you being nice to me?" He moves closer with my question.

"Let's just say I've decided to go for what's mine." His words send a surge through my chest as I realize he's talking about me.

"You don't get to say that." He moves his hand over my back and slides my hair away from my face before he leans in close.

"Sure I do, Kali." He slides his hand down, then back up as he sends chills through my body with his touch. He pulls my face toward his and begins kissing me.

He's being gentle, yet demanding. Like he wants to take his time, but expects me to meet him with every movement of his tongue. He tugs me onto him as he leans back, guiding me to straddle his waist.

His hands move fast over me, not allowing time for me to think about what's happening. He's Noah. All consuming and just as addictive as he always has been.

He slides the straps down on my tank top and lifts his head to kiss my chest. I love how his mouth feels on me and I'm screaming internally, hoping he'll slide the material lower and focus on my sensitive nipples.

"Fuck, Kali." His firm squeeze on my ass sends me even deeper into a swirl of delicate flesh that's more pathetic than I thought possible. I've wanted him for so long and he feels better under me than I imagined.

"Noah." I sit up and whisper his name while my body begins to take over. Even if I wanted to stop, I don't think I could at this point. I owe it to myself to explore what Noah and I have together.

# Chapter Eighteen
## Noah

I slide her tank top off and watch her nipples harden as the wind brushes over them. She's grinding her hips on my waist, making my dick hard and throwing my restraint out of control.

I want her more than I've ever wanted a woman in my life.

She reaches between her legs and tugs open the button on my jeans while I pull hers open. She lifts off of me just long enough for us both to drop our jeans, then we race to get back into the same position.

Our lips crash into each other, both of us biting and kissing like this is our last chance to live life. I feel her heart racing against my chest even though her tits brush against me every time she rotates her hips over me.

My dick glides through her wetness a few times before she stalls over me, searching my eyes. She pivots her hips and we stare into each other as she slides down the full length of my dick.

"Noah. Oh my god. You. Feel. So fucking good." She's breathy, speaking between thrusts as she moves over me.

This is what I've been missing my entire life. The intensity we have together is something I've never experienced and something I'm not willing to walk away from. She's mine. And someone I'll fight like hell to keep.

The wind blows through her hair and even though I'm fighting the urge to take over, I hold back and just watch her move over me. The slow grind of her hips and the tightness between her legs has me nearly going insane.

Her hands spread over my chest allowing her to shift, sending me even deeper inside her.

"Kali. Fuck." She lifts and drops her hips over and over until she's frozen in place allowing her orgasm to race through her, practically paralyzing her with the most satisfied expression on her face. She pulls her bottom lip between her teeth as she moans through the end of her release.

Once she falls on my chest and her hair

drapes over me, I take over. I spread both hands over her ass cheeks, giving me the grip I need to thrust into her slowly. I'm not in any hurry for this to end, so I'm making the most of every moment.

She starts to kiss over my chest and into my neck, softly biting every once in a while. Her skin is like silk against mine and the scent of her hair is even better this close.

I pull most of her hair into my grip, exposing her neck and chest to me when I tug her back to look at me. "You're making me crazy. I'll never be able to resist you after seeing you like this." My words slip out and the smile on her face shows me what effect they have on her. My dick takes over, sending me thrusting in and out of her with a fury until I'm forced to pull out and send my release all the way up her back.

She manages to get another release in before I finish, so we both come to a stop together, looking into each other's eyes while fighting for the breath that seems to escape us. I can feel her heart racing, matching my own while I come down from the high that she sent me to.

"Kali. I want you. Not just this, but all of you." My deep grumble seems to startle her into reality. She sits up abruptly, looking shocked by my words.

"That's what you say right now, but how will you be when we go back to the real world?" She moves off me with a quickness that sends a bolt of frustration through my body.

"What do I have to say to you to make you realize what I want?"

"I don't know, I guess your history with keeping your word isn't exactly clean when it comes to me." She uses my shirt to dry her back before she puts her own clothes on. I toss my shirt over my shoulder after she throws it at me.

"That's in the past."

"I guess I'll need to see that you've had a change of heart." She starts pacing the small area, her face looking horrified as the realization of what just happened hits her. "I can't believe I just did that with you." Tears begin to fall down her face and before I can get to her, she's crying out loud.

"Levi will hate me for this. How could I do this to him?"

"Wait, you were very clear about needing time to think about things. You two aren't a couple, so what's the issue?" I try to approach her only to have her walk away from me the second I get near.

"No we weren't a couple, but that doesn't stop the fact that I care about him. I don't want him to ever think that I was using him to get to you, because in all reality I wasn't. I really like spending time with him and I'm not even sure I want to stop. Jesus, this makes me sound like a whore!" She screams the last sentence before she takes off straight for the truck.

"No, it doesn't. It makes you sound like a confused woman who cares about two men." She turns abruptly to face be and uses her shirt to dry her own tears.

"Take me home please. I need to talk to Levi. And so help me if you try to beat me to it, I'll never speak to you again."

# Chapter Nineteen
## Kali

What have I done? Being near Noah has been something I've wanted my entire life and given the first chance, I take it, no matter the consequences to others. This makes me a monster and I'm terrified of what Levi will do once he finds out.

I can't swallow past the lump in my throat while Noah drives us home. He's still not wearing his shirt and that irritates me. "You have to put your shirt on."

"Excuse me, but I'm not going to slide on a cum filled shirt just to keep your little secret. I personally don't care if anyone thinks we just fucked."

"Noah. You're not going inside like that if he's home."

"Well princess, you'd better hope he's long gone." His attitude infuriates me and the lump in my throat turns into rage boiling at the base of my tongue.

"You're such an ass."

"Well, I've never claimed anything different and you know this about me, Kali."

"I know the real you. The ass is the one you show the world just to keep from getting hurt." He's putting up his walls again, I can feel him. Only this time I'm not going to race to try to get him to stop. I just made the biggest mistake of my life by fucking him. Now I can't think clearly to know if I'm coming or going.

How did I fall for two men? Both so different, yet both impacting me just as strongly. I can't be with one of them without thinking of the other. This is no way for me to live my life and it sure as hell isn't fair to them.

"Looks like you're safe. He's not home." I slam the door of the truck closed before he has a chance to finish his sentence. I don't have to be nice to him when he's acting like this. In fact, if he can't give me the time to clear things up with Levi, then that speaks volumes to me. I know where I stand. I must've been a challenge to him to get his hands on. He just wanted to prove that he could pull me away from Levi and mind fuck me at the same time.

"Look, Kali. This changes nothing. I still want you and I'll stop at nothing to make sure you realize that."

"Not now, Noah. You don't know what you want." I stop halfway up the stairs and turn to look at him. "Why don't you really think about what it is you want out of this before you completely turn my world upside down once again." And with that I turn and never look back. I close the door to Levi's room and the overwhelming rush of guilt sweeps over me while I try to gasp for breath.

"What have I done?" I slide down the door until I'm sitting against it, my tears falling faster than I can dry them. I'm wrecked with shame for allowing myself to get into this mess and I don't even know how to talk to Levi about what I've done.

I don't really have time to come up with a plan before there's a knock at the door. "Kali?" Levi's voice sounds unsure on the other side of the door and my body is in instant panic as I crawl to my knees and hold it closed.

"Levi. I just need a minute." I hear the sound of him sliding down the door on the opposite side, pulling me to match his action once again.

"I've got all day if that's what it takes." He's being nice and if he only knew why I'm upset, he wouldn't be sitting here with me.

"You need to just walk away. I'm no good for you."

"Why don't you let me make that decision?" His voice calms me even though it shouldn't. I'm about to make him see just how bad I really am for him.

"Look at this. She won't even let you in your own room." I stand the instant I hear Noah.

"Noah, stay out of this!" I yell as I open the door, causing Levi to fall back just slightly when I surprise him. Levi stands when Noah walks by with a giant smile on his face. I have the urge to follow him and slap it right off his face, but choose to stay and talk to Levi.

He closes the door behind him, leaving us

alone in his room once again. "I know this has been hard on you. I had some time to think this afternoon and wanted to talk to you about a few things." He starts in first, so I have to interrupt him quickly.

"I need to tell you something first." He flops down on his bed, looking me over and allowing me time to talk. Only I can't manage to get a word out of my mouth. I don't want to upset him and this is only going to do that.

"Kali, what's wrong? You have me worried."

There's no easy way to do this, but I know for a fact if I leave this room without doing it, Noah will be waiting to do it for me. If I have a single chance of Levi not hating me, this needs to come from me.

"Please don't hate me."

"I could never hate you, Kali."

"Levi, please let me finish before you say anything else. If I'm going to do this, I need to say it all at once." He nods slowly, obviously not assured he wants to know what I have to say.

"I'm completely stuck caring for two men. I came here a few weeks ago wanting to see Noah, then you came out of nowhere and showed me what it's like to be truly cared about. I've had so much fun with you and I can't tell you how much it means to me that you've protected me over and over again." I start pacing again. Not looking at him seems to make the words come out easier.

"Then Noah decided he wanted to stop fighting everything he's felt for me over the years. I told you both I need time to think, which is why I walked away from you this morning. I care about you both, Levi, yet all I seem to do is bounce from one of you to the other. It's not fair to you that I feel this way. Hell, it's not fair to me. It's gutting me inside to feel like this." I swallow hard, knowing this next part is going to be bitter tasting as I say it.

"I slept with Noah today." He sits up quickly and the instant hurt on his face is something I can't miss and even though he tries to shake it off fast, he doesn't succeed. "I went for a drive with him to talk and we stopped... and one thing led to another."

"I don't need the details, Kali." His words come out in a bite as he stands to face me. "I don't want to hear what happens with him." He looks down when he gets close to me, avoiding my eyes completely. I can feel him hurting and I hate it.

"You wanted space to see what there was there, I knew that. You've been very straightforward with me. Honestly, I'm surprised it took this long for you two to get to that point." He finally looks at me in the eyes and I let out the breath I've been holding.

"I only care about what you feel about me. About what we have together. And if you being with him has made you realize what you want." He slides his hands down both of my arms while we stand face to face. Chest to chest. Eye to eye.

"I can tell you I felt instantly guilty and worried about what I'd say to you. I can't lose you, Levi. You've been a friend to me like no one else. You've managed to break through all the walls I put in place specifically to keep everyone out." He turns away from me before he starts to talk.

"Friend, huh?"

"No we've been more than friends, but most importantly you've shown me what it's like to have someone loyal on your side and I've done nothing to repay you. I've only hurt you and brought chaos into your life."

"Don't you think I knew this shit with Noah was coming? He always gets what he wants, to hell with anything else." The look on his face is tearing me up again.

"I did this. I allowed this to happen. I don't know what I'm doing from one second to another with you two. On one hand, I have the man I've wanted my entire life and the other is a man I never knew existed." I walk closer to him, hoping he doesn't turn away from me before I get to make my point. "A man I never knew could care for me like he does. Make me feel loved with a simple touch." He doesn't turn away. "It's like you're teaching me to love myself, Levi. And that's confusing the shit out of me. It makes me realize maybe something I've wanted my entire life isn't what I need at all."

"Kali, I'll let you have the space you need to decide what you want, but I won't play games."

"I won't either. I'll always give you honesty."

"I can deal with that." He moves away from me once again, and this time the look of disgust is no longer spread across his face.

"I'm sorry, Levi." The lump is there the second I begin to say the words. I truly am sorry for the mess I've made.

"Just be honest like you said and I can handle everything else. I know you're working through some stuff." He doesn't say anything else before he wraps his arms around me, squeezing me tightly. We stand still while the rest of the world continues to proceed. I can hear his heartbeat against my ear as I lean my head on his chest.

I lean forward to kiss him, only to have him pull back. "But I won't be kissing your lips when you've just been with him. Take a shower. You'll have to wash that fucker off of you if you want anything from me."

# Chapter Twenty
## Levi

Things have been awkward at the house for the past few days to say the least. Kali stays to herself, rarely coming out of the guest bedroom when she's there.

She's been taking extra shifts at the club and seems to be extra focused on staying busy and unapproachable when I'm there. She's no different at home and has pushed Noah even further away.

The club is closed today, so she can't hide from me under the guise of work tonight. I don't like this shit and I want to talk to her about how this all went down. I get it. She feels guilty for being caught in the middle of what I want and what Noah is trying to claim.

What she doesn't understand is, I know it isn't her fault. I knew going into this that she has loved Noah since they were young. She's never even looked my way all these years. What started out as me trying to push Noah towards her, ended up with me falling for a girl I had no intentions of even liking. Now I'm caught up in this triangle of a disaster where it's inevitable that one of us is going to get hurt, if not all three of us.

My best friend who irritates the fuck out of me, but none the less is my family, has finally decided to let Kali get to him. By the looks of him lately, I'd say she succeeded. It's been days since I've acknowledged him, so to say shit is stressful here is an understatement. I'd feel better if I just knew where Kali's head was.

I'm still in bed, after working most of the night. It's nearly dark again, but I'm contemplating what I'll do on my night off when the doorbell rings. I don't move, knowing someone else will get it if I just ignore it. When it rings again, I throw off the covers and saunter downstairs, only to open the door to a pizza being held in my face.

"Pizza delivery for Kali." I look surprised as the guy reaches into his pocket for a pen. "Please sign here." I forge her signature and take the pizza to the bar. Opening the lid sends the scent of delicious greatness into my senses and I'm instantly tempted to tear into her pizza without even asking. I close the lid and take the pizza toward her room.

Her door is closed, but she must not hear my knock, leaving me with an easy decision to turn the knob and go in anyway. I'm not good with boundaries; I never have been. The fact that I've given her the space she's needed so far has shocked even me. So, she'll have to forgive me if pizza is my undoing.

I set the box at the foot of her bed and turn around when I hear something behind me. She's standing in nothing but a towel, allowing her wet hair to dangle over her right shoulder while she runs a brush through it.

"Awesome. I'm starving." Her eyes move straight for the box. "Do you want a piece?"

"Yeah. It smells amazing." The mixture of clean and pizza swirl in the room as she passes me. Her smell is familiar and suddenly something I cherish. I miss her in my bed and wish I could snap her out of her indecisiveness so I can spend my time sweeping her off her feet knowing I'm not confusing the shit out of her in the process.

She asked for space and I've given her that, but that doesn't seem to be getting any of us anywhere. She slips back into the bathroom before she steps out in a tank top and tiny shorts. Her tits move slightly as she walks toward the bed before she sits in the middle and crosses her legs. The giant piece of pizza she picks up doesn't have a chance when she starts in on it. I stand watching her and realize this may be the sexiest I've ever seen her. Real looks hot as fuck on her.

"You gonna stare at me eating or join me?" She looks at me over the piece in her hand before she bites down once again. "Nice underwear by the way. Did you really answer the door like that?" I look down and see nothing wrong with the way I'm dressed.

"Yes, I answered the door like this. The guy is lucky I wasn't lying naked when he rang."

She allows her eyes to slide down my chest and over my bulge before quickly taking her attention back to the pizza.

I sit beside her and sprawl out with my back against the headboard and my legs taking most of this side of the bed. She hands me a slice of pizza and follows my lead, leaning in almost the same position on her side.

It's a few seconds before either of us say anything. "Is this what you have planned for your night off?"

"Pretty much," she says with a full mouth.

"Sounds perfect to me." Well, partially perfect. I could think of a few things I'd like to add, but I won't go there yet. She's relaxing around me again and I'm not about to push her away when I have her like this. "Hit the remote and see if there's a movie on or something."

She finds a show and drops the remote between us before she grabs herself another piece of pizza. "You do realize this is like food porn to me." I look over at her, completely distracted by the way she looks next to me.

"Levi, this is not food porn."

"Oh really? Because I'm turned the fuck on right now and struggling to stay on my side of the bed." Well, there goes that space I was trying to give her. I may not have dove on top of her like I wanted, but I definitely altered the mood as I consumed her imagination with that porn comment.

"I thought you were mad at me." She sits up and shifts in the bed to face me.

"I'm not mad. Just giving you some space like you say you needed." I take another bite before I continue. "But I'm done with that shit." Her eyes challenge me as I speak. Playfully teasing as I can feel the effects of her watching me go straight through my body and into my dick.

"Thank you for the space."

"Did you get anywhere with that space? Do you have everything planned out for the rest of your life?" She picks at the meat on a piece of pizza sitting in the box.

"I'm not any clearer than I was the last time we talked." She dangles a pepperoni over her mouth before she uses her tongue to pull it in. Fucking with me even further and tempting me to lose my mind and the restraint allowing me to sit back to watch. I'm more of a do'er. She knows this.

"Well, I think this space shit is overrated. It hasn't helped. Maybe we should do things my way." She pops a piece of sausage in her mouth, chewing it slowly while she waits for me to finish what I'm saying.

"What's your way?"

I toss the last few bites of my pizza back into the box and shove the entire thing to the floor. Her eyes watch it land perfectly next to the dresser then she quickly squints in my direction. Climbing over her, she falls to her back, her head at the foot of the bed while I blanket her with my body. I kiss her slowly as she follows my lead and returns the kiss.

"Mmmm. You taste like pizza and cherry Chapstick. It's quite the combination." She smiles under me while I wrap my legs around her and straddle her waist. I sit up and slide my hands down her chest and over her arms, causing a heavy silence between the two of us. The intensity is almost immediately suffocating me as I wait for one single sign that she's fine with me attacking her like this. I'm trying to make a point, but of course if she says no, I'll stop immediately.

"Don't you think you should be between my legs for this to work out?"

"Oh. Is that what we're doing? This is me giving you space." I decide to tease her just a little, even though I want nothing more than to dive straight between her legs and take care of my sexual frustrations.

"Space may be overrated." She's not smiling anymore and I know I need to move quickly to keep her with me.

I slide her arms over her head as I lower my face to hers. "I think I have to agree. I like you much better up close."

"You're not so bad yourself like this, you know."

"We could be even closer if you'd like." She pulls her bottom lip between her teeth and still manages a smile before I kiss her and slide my own teeth over her lip instead.

"Mmmm. You're always so tempting." She moans and squirms beneath me, no doubt ready for me to slide between her legs and take this home. I adjust my body so that I'm between her legs.

She lifts them up, allowing me to slide her shorts off before she turns to her side. I slide in behind her and without another thought, I'm balls deep inside her, thrusting in and out. Rotating my hips and holding her against me feels perfect. *She* feels perfect against me. Her scent. Her touch. Even the sound she makes as I invade her without apology.

"Fuck, Kali," I whisper into her neck and grip it with one hand, using it as leverage as I pull her towards me over and over again. I needed this. I needed *her* and I have no plans to let her go this long without spending time with her again.

I miss Kali. I miss laughing with her and the fun we have even when we're being serious. If she still needs space, she's going to have to figure out a way to get it around spending time with me.

# Chapter Twenty-One
## Noah

Things are different since our drive the other day. She's been avoiding me, but to be fair she's been keeping her distance from everyone. I've been in my own head trying to figure out what I'm doing and how I want things to be with her.

I've loved her my entire life. Actually, I loved the woman I thought she was. I had no idea who she was and what she was capable of until recently and I have to say I'm loving this Kali even more. I just wish I hadn't waited until she fell for my best friend. This is ridiculous. I'm stuck thinking about her being with him possibly when he shouldn't even be in the picture.

This is what happens when you don't go after what's yours. Someone else will. And you have to be prepared to deal with the consequences.

I've been gone all day, on purpose. I knew she was home from work today and instead of her trying to hide from me, I thought I'd make it easy on her. Easy on me.

It didn't work. I'm more irritated now than I was to start with. I plan to talk to her tonight. She needs to know where I stand because I really haven't taken the time to tell her. It's hard to tell someone something when you're not sure yourself.

It's four in the morning by the time I pull into my driveway. The house is dark and I'm sure she's sleeping, so I pull out the whiskey and sit by the pool to think. The moonlight shines bright and flickers across the pool, pulling my attention towards the water as I continue to drink.

She's haunting me even as I sit here trying to understand her. How did it get to this? Kali has always been a weakness for me and now it seems she's mastered that to its fullest.

I drop back the last of my drink and pour another one before I head back inside. The house is quiet. So quiet that I'm not even sure anyone is here. Levi's truck is gone, so who knows.

Leaning on the bar I contemplate my next

step with her. Do I continue to avoid any contact with her in hopes of her one day coming to her senses about us? Or do I get in her face about us and force her to pay attention to me now that she has my undivided focus.

I've never been one to skirt around shit, so why am I doing that now. Swallowing the last of my drink, I drop it in the sink and head straight for her room.

I push open the door and see her curled up on one side of the bed, with the covers kicked off her. Her tiny figure barely takes up any room and I'm instantly itching to move in next to her. I watch her sleep for a few seconds before I close the door.

As I move closer, I quickly decide it's time to stop allowing her to ignore me and I'm sure as fuck about to do the opposite of avoiding her.

I pull my t-shirt over my head and drop it on the floor before I crawl up her bed from the bottom. She doesn't budge as I roll her over and slide my face between her legs. The t-shirt and panties she's wearing make it easy for me to get right into position.

I bite the lace covering her, causing her to startle. "You scared me." I move her shirt and blow slowly across her stomach until she lifts her hips just slightly.

"Sorry." Pulling her panties down her legs, I sit up and unbutton my pants. I waste no time pulling my dick out and there's no need to do anything to get me hard. I'm already there.

"Noah. I have to tell you something."

"No talking. Just let me take care of you." I slide my hands up her smooth legs until I have her ass in my hands. Lifting her hips, I lick her pussy once before I suck her clit until she's writhing against my face. She grips my hair and holds me in place while I work her over. Taking note of every sound she makes along with every squirm, I begin to learn what makes my Kali tick in the bedroom. What makes her crazy and what leaves her indifferent.

I quickly find that she prefers my more aggressive tendencies and when I take things a little further than the basic. She likes it rough and that thrills the fuck out of me.

Her death grip on my hair forces me to pleasure her until she's grinding herself through an orgasm from the efforts of my tongue. I move over her and take a handful of her hair, quickly noticing the dampness. She smells of shampoo and that makes me wish I would've made an appearance just a half an hour earlier. That shower could've been amazing.

"Have you been drinking." She smells the whiskey on me.

"I had two drinks when I got home." I move between her legs, my dick sinking in as she wraps her legs around my ass. "I was thinking about you."

"Oh you were." She lets out a breath when I thrust all the way in.

"Yes. I was trying to decide if I should leave you alone or remind you why we should be together." I thrust hard and deep. Slow and precise.

I hold her in my arms as I move in and out of her, kissing her as I do.

"Thought you said no talking." I bite her neck as I drive into her again. She moans and squeezes her legs the harder I bite. "Ahh. Fuckkkk." She likes it. The way she says *fuck* proves it.

We continue for hours. The sun begins to shine through the curtains before I decide to stop giving her orgasm after orgasm. We're both drenched in sweat as I begin to fuck her relentlessly allowing my own release to go over the edge. I roll us over and pull her against me, inhaling her scent again.

She wiggles against me, finding that perfect spot that we fit the best before she pulls my arm across her chest and holds it tight. "I love you Kali." I'm whispering the words before I have the chance to think about them. "I've always loved you."

# Kali

I've thought about this very situation most of my life. What would it feel like to have him hold me? Have him treat me like he can't keep his hands off me, then pull me in and tell me he loves me.

The only problem is… I'm in love with two men at the same time. Just when I think I can choose one over the other, they confuse me all over again. This isn't healthy for any of us. I'm turning into a whore allowing them both to fuck me in the same day. Thank god I had showered after Levi left, but I feel anything but clean.

I have to leave. I have to slip out of here and never look back because the thought of having to say goodbye to either of them isn't an option.

Slipping out of bed, I glance back to look at Noah's naked body. He's just as gorgeous as I imagined he'd be. The way he treated me tonight was perfect, but so was the way Levi fucked me. Levi spent time with me, laughing and joking, but still fucking me senseless over and over.

Then Noah comes in and does the same. I'm nearly sick to my stomach thinking about what I've become when I grab my things and slip out the door. The house is quiet and I leave it that way. I call a cab to meet me at the diner just down the road.

This is the best thing I could do for all of us. For Levi. For Noah. And For me.

I've decided to go home. I know I'll face the neighbor from hell and I'll lose that feeling of safety I've grown accustomed to, but I can't deal with the pull and push crap I've been doing with both Noah and Levi.

The truth is I can't decide which one I want to be with. I've tried. I've been thinking about both of them since I walked back into that house. What I've done to them and myself is unforgivable.

I thought Noah was the love of my life and now I'm not sure I wasn't destined to have two. The problem is, they're at the same time. I can't choose. And rather than breaking my heart to say goodbye to one of them, I'd rather face the danger of the psychotic neighbor from hell.

I've been saving every penny I've made to get me a car. I don't have enough to buy one as nice as my Jeep, but it'll have to get me something to get around in. My lease is up in two months and I'll move into a new house then.

I just need to work constantly and keep focused on moving forward. Levi and Noah will have to understand that I can't be around them anymore. It's too hard and I'm becoming consumed in guilt. It's killing me.

Tears slide down both my cheeks as soon as I sit in the cab. The drive to my house is quick and before I completely lose it, I'm inside with the water running in my shower.

Proof of Levi being here with me is still in my bedroom with the bed tore all to hell. I strip the bed and toss it all in the washer before I step into the shower, gasping for air as I remove them from my life completely.

My heart aches as I take in the overwhelming emptiness I feel now that I'm away from them. The void is suffocating me as the water rushes over my face and I can barely breathe. Before I know it, I'm squatting with my legs tucked against my chest allowing the hot water to wash away the tears that fall. My guttural cries echo in the bathroom, only making me sound more pathetic than I feel.

I remain this way until the hot water runs out. When the cold takes over, I'm no longer able to cry. Shivering takes over and I fight through it and just accept the shock to my body. This is better than feeling all the agony I was before.

When I can't take another second of the cold, I crawl to the faucet and turn off the water. My breathing is rapid as I try to regain the warmth I lost. The towel in my hair and the robe around my body only does so much to help.

I catch a glimpse of myself in the mirror and have to stop and look again. I look as bad as I feel and that's a problem because I need to be at work in a couple of hours. If either of them show up to ask me questions, I don't want them to think I regret my decision to leave. It's apparent neither of them are going to make this easy on me, so I need to be ready to stand my ground.

One thing I've learned about them both is they are stubborn, but they are also both protective. That's something I've always known though. It just seems to have come out in full force lately with everything going on in my life.

I force myself to put on makeup and do my hair, hoping that will make me feel half alive. The music in the background helps slightly until a song comes on that reminds me of Levi. I rush to turn it off and fight back the tears that start to surface again.

Glancing at my phone, I can see that they're both awake now. Message after message and missed calls line up my screen from both of them. I refuse to read any of them and I sure don't have it in me to listen to the voice messages they've left.

I call the cab service early, hoping if I'm at work they'll both leave me alone. That'll give me time to get the strength up to push them both back when they approach me to come back. I can't even say who I think I'll see first after the way they both acted yesterday, but I know they won't give up until they've said their peace.

My shift ends early tonight, which will give

me time to get home and settled in before it gets dark. I look around the curtain as I wait for my ride, studying the neighbor's house. Everything is frozen in place as I look for any signs of life over there. There aren't any vehicles in his driveway, so I can only assume he's not there either.

I only allowed myself a quick glance when the first cab dropped me off, wanting to get inside before he drove off. My house is secure, even more so since Levi had a new security system installed. I guess he felt better knowing if I ever came back here, I'd be protected.

The rumble of an engine gets louder and my heart begins to beat rapidly. I look in the neighbor's driveway expecting it to be him, but it's still empty. It only takes a few seconds and the knob on my door is being turned. "Kali. I'm coming in." It's Levi. Before I have a chance to say anything back to him, he's standing in my living room.

"What the fuck? You have a key to my house?"

"Yes. I'm not fucking around with that

asshole next door. I told you I don't want you staying here." He's livid as he paces the room.

"Levi. I can't do this anymore. You're both making me crazy and I don't like who I've become."

"Don't be ridiculous. You're perfect and I've watched you smile more in the past few weeks than you probably have in years."

"I'm not perfect. Do you not know that I slept with Noah an hour after you left my bed? What does that make me, Levi?" I'm yelling hysterically when my cab pulls up. Levi steps back in shock before he tries to move to stop me from leaving. "No. Don't touch me. I told you I can't do this anymore. Let me go, Levi."

The look on his face breaks me. I turn quickly, because if I stay any longer I'll lose what little control I have over my emotions. "Lock the door when you leave!" I yell back as I practically run to the car waiting for me. He's glaring at me as the cab pulls away and even though I should feel better about getting away that easily, I know he'll be back to make his point.

# Chapter Twenty-Two
## Levi

She's impossible. Putting herself in danger because she's caught up in a mess with the two of us. I know what I need to do. This can only be settled after I talk to Noah. He can't want this for her. I've never seen her more torn than she was just now.

I lock up her house and call Greg. He's the friend I've had watching this fucking neighbor of hers. Luckily, He answers on the first ring.

"Tell me you have him in your sights."

"Sure do. Also have some footage of him breaking into a house a few streets over. I'm sending that to a friend of mine on the force. He should be out of your hair soon."

"Nice work. Keep me posted today. Kali has moved back to her house, so I'll need to know everything that happens today." She doesn't know I've had this guy tracked. It was something I had to do. I couldn't handle the thought of this guy coming around her. Something tells me he'll try to prove a point if he ever gets his hands on her.

"Will do." Greg is a guy I knew from the club. He started his own security company a few months ago and was thrilled to get my call. I knew he'd do what it took to get that fucker out of Kali's life.

I know she's headed to work. She'll be safe there, so I'm going to spend the next few hours trying to reason with the only other person who doesn't seem to listen to me when I talk. This should be fun.

He's rushing down the stairs when I open the door. He stops to look at me frantically before he starts asking questions. "Did you find her? Is she safe?"

"Yes. She's at work. Mike just texted me saying she came in early." He moves at a normal speed down the remaining steps and follows me into the living room. I sit on the couch and wait for him to sit in the chair across from me.

"So you fucked her last night." He stands abruptly, anger spreading across his face.

"What I do with her is none of your fucking

business."

"It is when it causes her to run out of here, straight toward a fucking sicko that lives near her." I put my arm over the back of the couch while he slowly sits down again. "She made it my business when she told me through her tears, saying that she had been with you an hour after I left her bed." He squints his eyes at me, processing what I've just said.

"She's torn between the two of us. I could tell by the way she ran from her house to keep from having to look me in the face." He places his elbows on his knees and leans forward in a thinking position.

"We have to make this easy on her. One of us needs to walk away."

"Just who do you suggest does that?" He stands again when I question his motives.

"She's always loved me."

"And you've always pushed her away." I interrupt him, only to have him do the same right back to me.

"Let's not talk about how idiotic I've been

over the years. I think we can both admit to stupid moves in our past."

"I care about her and can't stand seeing her like this." I swallow around my words while I realize I just stopped myself from saying that I love her. That's something I should say to her before I say it to anyone else.

"I've loved her as long as I can remember." He says it as if he's been a Saint all these years and deserves her.

"We can sit here and have a pissing contest, or we can do something to help her find that happiness again. She deserves that."

"It seems like she can't make a decision when it comes to the two of us." Noah moves to the kitchen and pours himself a drink. I take mine back as soon as he hands it to me. "So I guess we do need to make it easy on her."

"How exactly do you plan to do that?" I know what I want to suggest, but I'm sure he won't like my idea.

"You can disappear and make my life easy." His evil smile has me trying to decide if he's being serious or if he's just testing me."

"Or you could go back to being your asshole self and push her away like you're bound to do soon anyway." He stops smiling and stares at me as if he's just now realizing that I don't have any intention of stepping back on this one.

"Are you willing to walk away to allow her to be happy?" He speaks to me as if I haven't already contemplated this exact scenario. "Because if that's what it takes, I'll go." He surprises me with his statement. I didn't expect him to be selfless when it came down to it. It's honestly not in his nature.

"Seems as though we would both go to extremes to make her happy." I walk back into the kitchen and refill my glass with whiskey. "So how do we choose?"

"We need to spend time with her together. We'll be able to tell who she's drawn to more and the other one will need to disappear once we decide." I throw that out there, knowing it'll still be difficult to decide. She's drawn to both of us and I can see her happy just hanging out with both of us at the same time. But I guess that'll depend on how easy it is to convince her to meet with us at all. She may be pissed and make it impossible to see what she wants. "She's determined to stay away from us."

"Well, then we go to her. When have we ever waited for anything to come to us?" I like how his mind is working and I know instantly what we have to do. "We'll be at her house tonight when she gets there. This is it. Winner takes all." He walks out of the room like he's on a mission and my mind instantly begins to think about how the evening will go.

I need to call in to work. There's no way in hell I'm missing a single second of this night. I need to be in control of how things go and watch my own back. If there's one thing I know about Noah, it's that he'll stop at nothing to get what he wants.

*This should be one hell of an interesting night.*

# Chapter Twenty-Three
## Noah

I knew something was wrong with her last night. I wanted to leave all the stress behind us and enjoy my time with her, but it seems as though it just caused the problems to grow and now she's moved out.

Levi said he cares about her, but I know what he was really trying to say. He hasn't been the same since she came into this house. For one thing, he hasn't brought a single woman home since she came into our lives again. That alone speaks volumes about where he's at in his head. I've known him long enough to say he's used to four or five women in a week at times. He likes to play and that's something that stopped the second she arrived.

What pisses me off the most is I can see she feels the same about him. The way she looks at him is the way she used to only look at me. Now I'm sharing those perfect expressions with my best friend.

I have only myself to blame. If I would've

allowed myself to be true to how I felt that first night, none of this would be happening. This would all be going in a completely different direction. Who knows, I may have ended up pushing her away after admitting my feelings, just like I always have. Maybe seeing the two of them together has made me fight for what I deserve for once in my life; which was what Levi was screaming at me to do. Maybe I just don't want him to have her if I can't. I've always been one for a challenge.

The hot water feels amazing as I shower and think about how I want tonight to go. We need it to be as normal as possible. Stay in and cook together, maybe watch TV or play some games. The best way to really see how she feels is to get her tipsy and see what she says. I've always said there's a truth to what people say when they're under the influence.

I finish my shower and get ready quickly, knowing there's a lot I want to do today. The first will be checking out that fucking neighbor of hers. If I end up having to be the one to walk away from all of this, I want to make sure she's safe.

Levi is standing in the kitchen when I go downstairs. "I'm going to get stuff to cook out on the grill, do you need anything from the store?" I decide to let him know what I've planned for the night. "I figured we could just chill at her house. Do the shit normal people do and drink a little. It's probably long overdue for us again anyway." He nods at me as checks his phone.

"I have that fucker under surveillance, he's about to be hauled off to jail for breaking into a house just down the road from Kali's. I'm not sure if it'll happen before she gets home or not, so we can't be late getting over there."

"Maybe one of us should drive her home. I'd like to see him come in with us there. I might actually enjoy ripping out his insides after the way this day is going." He looks up at me and smiles as if he can relate. I'm guessing he can.

"I'll get her from the club and meet you over there." He pushes off the cabinet and follows me to the door. "Tonight is the night. Looks like one way or another you'll be rid of me." He throws that out just as I close the door. I notice the jolt of his words as I take them in.

I may have wanted to choke him at times, but truth be known, he's the only real friend I've had. He's put up with me at my worst, which has been more often than not.

A somber feeling washes over me as I drive away from the house. My life will change after tonight. One way or another I'll be saying goodbye to at least one person I care about.

# Kali

My shift seems to fly by and before I realize what time it is, it's time for me to go. I didn't have the time to call the cab yet, so I pull out my phone to do it.

I notice a message from Levi saying he's in the parking lot to give me a ride home. When I found out that he called in to work, I had hoped he'd decided to leave it alone for today. I should've known better. He's determined and the only way to get him to leave me be is to be even more stubborn and bullheaded than he is.

Walking out the door and into the parking lot, I see him immediately. My heart sinks as I look at his face. He doesn't approve of me distancing myself, but I didn't think he would.

I slide in and feel the heaviness between us. "You didn't have to pick me up. I can call a cab."

"We need to talk anyway." He comes back with a quick response. Not one that I'm used to from him.

"Levi. Please don't make this harder on me than it already is. I can't choose between you two and I refuse to be the reason you both hate each other."

"Noah and I came to an understanding today. Everything's going to work out just fine." He starts moving the truck toward the exit.

"What does that mean?"

"It means we aren't letting you go without spending some time with you first. We need to know your house is safe and the best way for us to do that is for us to be there." He turns right before he continues. "That'll give me some time

to make sure that asshole next door is out of
your way for good."

I don't ask him what he means. He's been
working on that for a few days now. "I haven't
seen him yet."

"Well I'm not going to let there be a yet,
Kali. I don't care how pissed off you get."

"All right. I'll let you take me home, make
sure I'm safe, then you have to leave." He
doesn't respond. I pull out my phone and look at
my messages from both of them this morning.
Seeing how demanding Noah was in these, I'm
honestly surprised there wasn't two of them in
the parking lot waiting for me.

We pull into the driveway and I see that
Noah is sitting in his car waiting on me to get
home. My nerves flare up instantly and I can only
imagine the confrontation they're both about to
have. I open my door and decide to head straight
into the house.

I need to prove to them that I'm fine to
stay here, then make them both leave. "Please.
Come in and see for yourself. I'm fine. No one is

here and then you can both go home. I don't want to talk about anything with either of you right now."

"My dear, we aren't here to talk. We don't plan to leave anytime soon either. You're going to let us make dinner and we're going to have a night in at your house for a change." I look at Noah with curiosity, wondering what they're both up to.

"I left you both this morning for a reason."

"And what the hell was your reason?" Noah snaps back as he sits the bags of groceries on the counter.

"I don't like myself lately. You two have me confused and this isn't going to help." I sit on a barstool in defeat, knowing they'll both be impossible tonight if I don't just let them do their thing and make dinner. I'm leery of their intentions and watch for any clue as they move around the kitchen.

"Why wouldn't you like yourself? You have two men who both care about you. Do you know how many women would jump at the chance to spend an evening with us?" Noah continues to parade around the kitchen acting like this is a normal night for us, while Levi begins to chop the onions.

"Well if you ask me, the pressure is overrated." They both look at me simultaneously. Since I can't decide which one to direct my attention to, I chose to move my focus to my hands as I fold them together on the counter.

"You just need to stop stressing. Tonight is only fun and relaxation. Leave all your worries for tomorrow." Noah again, trying to make me forget about the triangle I've gotten us into.

"What are you two up to?" Levi looks up at me, innocently batting his eyes before he responds.

"We're cooking you dinner. Maybe if you're lucky, we'll beat you in a board games before we leave." I'm not sure if I believe either of them, but for now I'm just going to enjoy spending time with them one last time. Before the night is over, I'm going to tell them both where I stand. I have to walk away from them and they have to let me go.

I glance over at Noah and watch him pour three glasses of whiskey, topping them all off with a little coke. He slides one my way and another toward Levi. *Since when do these two get along like this?* I'm trying my hardest to just enjoy it, but I'm having a hard time believing that they've just magically decided to get along.

Taking back the drink quickly, I end up choking on the potent fire sliding down my throat. They both watch me move around the room as they continue to prepare the food. It's as if they're suffocating me. "I'm going to take a shower. I smell like a bar."

I take this opportunity to walk out of the room and get some breathing space. It's going to take a minute for me to get my thoughts together and figure out what I'm going to do with these two stubborn asses. I lock the door to my bedroom and the bathroom just to make sure neither of them get any bright ideas. I wouldn't put it past either one of them to bust in on me.

Being in the kitchen with both of them only

made me feel worse about what I've done. They are best friends and have been for years. Yes, they get on each other's nerves just like brothers would.

I can't be the person that comes between them and it's inevitable if I choose one over the other. My shower is hot and steamy, just like I like it. I stay in longer than I plan to, but it does wonders to help me get some clarity.

If they want a normal evening where we pretend like things are going to work out, then I'll give them that. But after this, I'm having my locks changed and forcing them both to stay away. Maybe if I break down and scream at them like I feel like doing, they'll leave me alone.

Putting the least amount of effort into my hair, I brush it and pull it up in a messy bun while it's still wet. I don't add any makeup, the last thing I'm trying to do tonight is impress anyone. I roll down the waistband of my sweatpants, trying to keep them up on my hips. It's past time for me to do some laundry, so I throw everything from my bag into a pile and pick it up. If they want a normal night, then I can't think of anything more appropriate than doing my laundry.

# Chapter Twenty-Four
## Noah

She walks out here looking sexy as fuck, silencing both Levi and I at the same time. A tiny pair of lace panties hangs from the bottom of the pile of clothes in her arms and I recognize them as the pair I pulled off of her just last night. She catches me staring and only allows herself to look at me for a second. It's obvious that she's doing her best to avoid both of us tonight, which won't help us see who she's better connected to.

"How do you want your steak?" Levi manages to pull her attention for about the same length of time that I did.

"Medium rare." Her messy hair fucks with my mind as I start to think what it would be like if I took a large handful of it and pulled her back against me while I fuck her from behind. I close my eyes and drink the last of my beer, even though it's not my drink of choice.

We plan to keep our wits about us tonight, but still manage to get her to relax. The way she's acting stiff, I'm afraid it's going to be more difficult than we anticipated.

Levi steps outside to put the steaks on and I take the opportunity to get a point across to Kali. Stepping up behind her as she drops the last few items in the washer, I surprise her with the pressure of my body against hers. She's up against the washer, allowing me to grind my hips into her ass. Her breathing halts with a sharp inhale as she glares at me from over her shoulder.

"Noah, I can't. You can't."

"I don't do well with orders." I grip that mess in her hair and pull her back against me just like I imagined. It's so much better than I had in my head. Her scent consumes me and I'm instantly wishing Levi wasn't about to come through that back door again.

I grip her hip with the other hand, forcing her against me completely. "Fuck, you make me crazy. If you think you can just walk away from this, then you're obviously stronger than I am." I release the grip on her hair to slide my hand over her neck. She extends as if she's inviting me to squeeze tight, so I do while I kiss the shoulder that she's made so available to me.

"This tiny fucking tank top isn't going to help your little crusade." I look down the front of her top, the shape of her tits teasing me perfectly. My dick is hard by now and I want nothing more than to carry her over my shoulder straight into her bedroom, fuck her senseless and make her stop running from me.

"Noah, you have to stop." Her whisper brushes across my face as she exhales through her own fight. She's attempting to prove restraint, when I want no part of that shit.

The sound of the back door has her pushing me away. I smile as she works to compose herself and pretends I didn't just fuck with her mind. I should feel guilty for what I just did, but I don't. If either of them think that I'm about to just stand back and let the woman I love go again, they're both out of their fucking minds.

Levi looks at me suspiciously. His

squinting glare tells me I'm about to meet my match in this little game he suggested we play. It's a good thing I'm not afraid to pull at her darkest desires. Something tells me what we have is a little more scandalous than anything they've ever had together. Her voyeurism that first night is my proof of that.

# Levi

It appears I'm going to have to play dirty, even though we both said we wouldn't. Noah obviously did something while I was outside, because I've become very familiar with that flustered look on Kali's face. She was turned on when I walked in. Who knows what he said or did to make her switch her mood so quickly.

I'm going to need some tequila if I'm going to be able to go head to head with that fucker tonight. Deep down, I just want to kick his ass and end all of this, but I know that isn't going to keep Kali from pushing us both away. She doesn't want the stress and that would put her over the edge. I know her well enough to make that assumption.

"Noah, why don't you take these out to the grill and season the steak while you're at it." I hand him the foil wrapped vegetables and the seasoning. The smirk on his face is challenging, but I ignore him. Luckily he takes the tray from me and goes out the door.

"You doing all right?" I choose to show her respect and compassion. Something I'm sure he knows nothing about.

"Not really." Stepping in her path, I stop her from leaving the room. Her eyes bolt to mine and we both stay frozen in place until I slide my hands down her arms.

"You have nothing to be stressed about. Just relax and have some fun with us tonight. Just be you." She wraps her arms around my waist and I inhale the fresh scent of her hair just under my chin as I pull her in for a hug. My arms are still around her when Noah barges through the door.

She doesn't move too quickly from my arms and I'm almost positive Noah growled under his breath as he rinsed the tray.

"I'm thinking we should play some poker tonight. Who's in?" She steps back and shrugs before she responds to Noah.

"I've never played. You guys will have to teach me."

"It's easy, but if you lose you have to take something off." She laughs as Noah attempts to draw her in with strip poker.

"I don't think so. You two can play and I'll watch."

"I bet we can convince you to join us." His smile causes her to look down. He's coming on strong and I can't tell if his game is going to work on her or push her further away. I sit next to her and run my hand down her back. She squirms as my touch slides over her ass. A quick smile and a glance from her tells me she didn't hate that I just did that.

"So your plan is to feed me and get me drunk, then what?" She looks to Noah before turning to me again.

"We're just here to enjoy some time with you. And to make you see that we're okay with whatever decision you make. We aren't here to pressure you into anything."

"Yes. We aren't here to make you choose, but if you're having a hard time letting go of someone you say you've loved most of your life, we understand." I look up at Noah and watch him give her his panty dropping smirk that I've seen him use time after time.

"You two are fucking making me crazy. I can't deal with this crap tonight. Can you both just go?" She shocks me as she stands up and yells at the both of us.

"No can do, sweetheart."

"I'm suffocating. Do you not see what you're doing to me?" She starts crying before she completely loses her shit on us. "Noah. You have no boundaries. I wanted you to be like that when I first came to you, but you had to play your fucking games, leading me right into his arms." She shifts her look to me as she continues to back away from both of us. Her hands flailing as she yells.

"Arms that made me feel safe and loved for the first time in years. Then you couldn't fucking just let me be, you had to come at me with your mind fuck, telling me now. NOW you're in love with me and you want to see what we can be together." She walks toward Noah, stabbing him in the chest as she continues. "I was happy. I was safe. I felt loved. And then you changed all of that by reminding me what I've loved about you for all of these years." She turns away from him, her shoulders falling as if she's defeated. "You made me leave the security I had with Levi and threw me into this unknown shit. Now I can't breathe because I can't hurt Levi. I can't handle how it feels when he's not a part of my life now." She turns toward me, her tears clawing at my heart as I watch her come undone.

"But I can't stand going a day without talking to you either, Noah. No matter how hard I try to stay away from you, I can't. Don't you see what this is doing to me?"

We both stand motionless, taking in everything she says. "This is why I have to let you both go. I can't choose. I'll be miserable if I do." She rushes out of the room, leaving us both speechless, frozen in our stance as we contemplate how the hell to proceed from here.

"I refuse to walk away, Levi. It's Kali." He speaks to me as if I'm not aware of who she is or how important she is to him. The problem is, he's not remotely aware just how much she means to me.

"I'm not going anywhere. For the first time in my life, I've found love. I found someone worthy of my love and loyalty. If you think I'm going to walk away and make this easy on you, you have another thing coming." He isn't happy to hear my response. "Yet here we are fighting over her like she's ours to fight over. It really doesn't matter what we're willing to do when she's running from both of us."

"You do realize we only have one option that will allow us all to get a fraction of what we want. Let me get the steaks and we'll talk." Not

sure where his mind is going,  I move to the bar
stool to hear him out.

# Chapter Twenty-Five
## Kali

I need fresh air. Stepping outside seems to help with that, even though this is something I normally don't do here. I'm walking down the driveway to get my mail, when I see the neighbor's truck coming down the road. My heart sinks and I'm instantly terrified. I rush as fast as I can back into the house, only to be met at the door by both Noah and Levi.

They're both on guard and ready to annihilate anything that's chasing me, only to see there's nothing running after me. "What the fuck is happening?" Noah steps outside to see the neighbor pulling up in his driveway. "Did he do something to you?"

"No. I just didn't want to be outside with him."

"This is what we're talking about. You can't fucking be here with this man living next door to you." Levi spins me around so that his back is to the door and I'm between the two of them.

I look over Levi's shoulder and I see the sicko standing on my porch. He must have a death wish coming up here with these two guys here. That or he's fishing for them to do something again. "Look what finally decided to come home." His disgust for me is obvious the second he opens his mouth. "Do you really think I don't know you're having me followed?" I look at him confused while he starts to move toward the steps.

"The next fucking step you take will be your last if it's in the direction of this house. You need to get your ass out of here before I remind you why you should." Levi is quicker on his feet than Noah is, but both of them meet the guy before he has a chance to take another step.

"I haven't had you followed." I try to reply to him in hopes that he'll leave.

"I have," Levi speaks up, his deep voice practically a roar as he dives for the guy. Noah jumps to help as well. They're punching the guy over and over and I'm instantly worried they won't stop before it's too late.

"Please stop," I begin to cry out, only to have them all ignore me. They both continue to pummel the guy into the ground and during all of the chaos of trying to get them all to stop, I miss a man running from the street to break it up.

There's blood all over the neighbor and both Levi and Noah are taking turns getting a few more shots in before the guy from the street pulls Levi off of him.

"Greg, get this fucker out of here." Levi pulls away from being held, his chest heaving from anger as he leans over, lifts then tosses the neighbor into the arms of the man from the street. Levi is bleeding on his cheek and after a quick glance over Noah, I can see that he is too. I just can't tell how bad their faces are hurt.

"I'll take care of him. You two get cleaned up. I may need you to come in to the station to file a report in the morning. But hopefully I have all the footage I'll need. There's already a warrant out for this asshole. I just need to take him in." This Greg guy is huge and has no problem dragging the neighbor to his car.

I stand in shock as the two men I care about most glare at the man who has scared me for months. My heart beats rapidly as I come down from the panic that had me worried one of them would kill him and I'd lose them forever.

"Jesus. You both scared the shit out of me." I move closer to them both, not sure who I should hug, so I don't approach either. "Come inside. We need to get you cleaned up to see how bad your injuries are." I walk into my bathroom to get the supplies I need to stop the bleeding. Neither one of them says anything as they follow me.

Both of them sit on the edge of my bed, facing me while I rush around the room to open the gauze and ointment so I can clean their wounds.

"You had him followed?"

"Yes. I told you I'd make sure you're safe." Levi melts my heart as he admits to ensuring my safety. I take an antiseptic wipe and touch both of them at the same time. Both injuries seem to be a small cut that will be easy to heal once the bleeding stops.

"Here. Hold this." I get them to put pressure on their own cuts. The way they're both looking at me isn't fair, so I step back. Levi stands quickly, pulling me into his arms.

"All I want is for you to be safe and happy." I smell his cologne even over the sweat and dirt on his t-shirt from the fight. Tucking my hands behind his waist, I give in and let him hold me. It feels amazing to be in his strong arms like this. I'm positive he's holding me tighter than he has in the past.

Extra hands slide down my arms, surprising me instantly. "That's all we both want." I look over my shoulder and see Noah standing right behind me. I turn to face him and he wraps his arms around me too, both of them surrounding me with strength and love while I try to swallow around the lump in my throat.

"Thank you both." I push Noah back and step out from between them. "You have no idea how much fun I've had over the past few weeks. You've reminded me what it's like to be loved.

Both of you have." I look between them as I talk.

They both take a step forward at the same time, each sliding a hand down one of my arms as they pull me toward them. "Maybe you've been looking at this all wrong." Noah talks next to my ear and I listen as their closeness paralyzes me.

"Maybe you don't have to choose one of us." Levi continues the conversation in the other ear, their breaths heating up my neck from both sides.

"You can have both of us." Noah bites my ear just as he finishes the words that surprise me. I try to step back from them, but they both keep me in place.

"Stop running from us. Just let us love you." Levi tries to calm me even though my mind is going crazy trying to imagine what made them come to this conclusion.

"You're both out of your mind. You expect me to believe you want to share me?"

"We decided it's a better compromise than losing you forever," Levi tries to explain before

Noah pulls me against him and moves me so that my back is against Levi.

"We will share you. You'll have us both as long as you want us," Noah whispers against my mouth. They've surrounded me, completely enveloping me into a warmth I could never explain. Both of them are touching me in the most tender way as they try to get their point across.

Levi turns me to face him, forcing me to look into his eyes. Noah slides in behind me, again allowing me to feel completely cherished. "This is the only way for you to be happy. We both see it, now you just need to come to terms with it and move back in with us." I watch his eyes dance around as he waits for me to respond. When I don't, Levi moves in for a kiss. A deep kiss that's meant to show me how he feels about me. One that I find myself returning even though I feel the guilt of Noah being behind me.

I pull away. "Wait. I can't stand feeling like I'm jumping between your beds. I hate the guilt

I've been living with."

"Shhhh." Levi places his finger over my lips.

"No guilt. Just happiness and pleasure like you've never experienced," Noah speaks against my ear, sending a chill over my body. I lean my head against his chest and give in when he starts to run his hands up my torso, getting closer to my chest with each breath.

"Kali, you deserve to be loved." I watch Levi speak to me as Noah's hands send heat across my body. "And to love who you want. You deserve to have everything you've ever wanted." He stalks toward me, speaking deeply as Noah steps back, allowing Levi to pursue us slowly. His gravel voice is getting sexier with every step. "You deserve to be safe. To walk into your home and have your pick of strong arms to run to." Levi reaches behind his head and lifts his t-shirt over his head.

Noah stops moving us, allowing me to touch Levi's chest while I hear him pull his own shirt off. I kiss Levi's chest and allow him to slide my tank top over my head, his hands brushing down my sides.

My back is bare, Noah not covering me immediately. He finally steps in behind me and slides my elastic gathered hair off my shoulder, giving him the access he needs to shoot chills through my body with his bite. Noah moves slowly, sliding a silk scarf over my chest before he blindfolds me, tying it tightly behind my head.

"Just feel us, Kali," Levi speaks against my lips again and I inhale his scent. Masculine. Sexy. Levi.

"I feel you." I sound breathy and pathetic, but completely consumed in these men. My men, if I so choose to take them up on their offer. Not that I can imagine saying no to what they're suggesting so far.

Noah's hand slides inside my pants as he wraps his arms around me from behind. Levi tugs the elastic out of my hair, allowing my still wet hair to fall over my shoulders once again. Noah pushes my pants down my legs, letting them fall to the floor and leaving me naked between two men for the first time in my life.

Levi pulls his buckle open and kicks his pants and shoes out of the way before he moves against me. Noah does the same and before I know it, Levi has my legs wrapped around his waist and he's slowly gliding his dick inside me. Noah stands solid as if he's a wall that Levi begins to fuck me against.

Wrapping my hands into Noah's hair as he stands behind me, I begin to ride Levi. Rotating my hips as I find a way to squeeze and clench my muscles, making myself tight enough to pull a few groans out of Levi. Noah holds me up with his hands on my tits while Levi grips my thighs.

So many strong arms surround me with fingers sliding over my body. Mouths and tongues leaving a trail of moisture, pulling me at an insane speed straight into a whirl of sensation. I won't make it long with these two. I never have one on one, so I know I won't with both of them working me over. They have me wrapped around their every move and I can't help but wish I could see them. I want to watch their faces.

Levi walks me to the bed before he sits me down carefully. I feel the bed dip behind me and before I know it, I'm in the middle of the bed, sandwiched between both of them. I lie on my back and let the chaos of both of them consuming me take over my body. It's like nothing I've ever experienced, leaving me paralyzed to their touch.

Noah pulls me toward him at the same time Levi gets closer to my back. "Kali, tell me you don't want us both at the same time and we'll stop." I can't tell them that because the truth is, now that I'm thinking about it, I want it bad.

"I want." Noah thrusts inside me, making me gasp and stop talking at the same time. "I want you both." It's as if the second the words leave my mouth, I flip a switch on both of them. A switch where the two of them move in sync and position me so that they can both enter me. Noah shifts his hips so that he's deep inside me before Levi stands on the bed, guiding my head to suck his cock.

"Get it nice and wet, baby." Noah slides his fingers inside my ass, slowly making me frantic as I imagine what it'll be like when Levi actually fills me completely. He stretches me perfectly as he fucks me while I gag and take Levi to the back of my throat. "That's it." He pops the tip against my tongue a few times before he moves in behind me.

Everything freezes, including my breathing as Levi slides in slowly, only entering a short distance with each thrust. The burning sensation as he continues to stretch me is both painful and a pleasure as I allow my body to relax. "You're fucking beautiful. Those damn lips are already swollen." I feel how puffy they are and how tight my chest is as they move me. My nipples are hard and every sensation I have seems to be rushing straight to my core.

"That's it." Levi begins to move faster with each thrust and I can't internalize how they're making me feel any longer. My moans turn into screams of pleasure as they rock my fucking mind.

This is wrong, I know it, but I can't seem to drum up an ounce of guilt. To me, this is perfection and love at its finest. Both of them, worshipping my body with their delicious mix of rough and tender touches can't possibly be immoral. And if it is, save me a seat, between them, in Hell. I refuse to deny myself anything that feels this damn good.

We have sex for hours. Both of them making it their mission to make my collapse in exhaustion when they finish. I've always fantasized of having a threesome, but never imagined it becoming a part of my everyday life. Is it even a possibility that they're really okay with this situation? Could we really coexist as if we're a trio? Will they get mad at me if I spend too much time with one of them over the other?

I pull off the blindfold and smile as I slide between them. We all lie on our backs, breathing deeply as we let the sweat drip down our bodies. This makes me anxious the more I think about all the possible ways this could go wrong. This is something we need to have a serious talk about.

One that I need to be included in this time.

"You both want me to believe that you won't get mad at me if I spend more time with one of you over the other?"

"We know you'll be with both of us." Noah throws his arm over his face and exhales. "We just need you to be you. Do what you want and who you want at all times. If you're happy, then we're happy." He throws out the expectations as Levi slides his fingers between mine.

Noah rolls over to face me, placing a soft kiss on my shoulder before he continues. "No, really. We understand what this means. I know you're mostly worried that I'll be an angry ass when you spend time with him, but I won't."

"And I won't hold it against you if you roll with that ass over there." Levi kisses my other shoulder, sending a smile across my face.

"Yeah, yeah. I think I proved my worth to this little trio we have here. Say what you want." Noah falls back on his back again, covering his face again.

Levi slides out of bed and I watch him

walk naked out of my room. "Where are you going?" I sit up, planning to follow him out of the room.

"To eat. My ass is starving."

# Epilogue
## Kali

"You're gorgeous, stop fussing and get back in bed with me." Levi has become demanding since I moved back in. Noah was already ridiculous, so between the two of them, I'm surrounded by alpha personalities constantly. It's a good thing I can handle them both. I just choose to pick my battles.

"You have to say that." I sit on the edge of the bed only to have him crawl over me and slide me under him. His muscular body covers mine while he takes it upon himself to trail kisses down my neck.

"I don't have to say anything. Mmmm, fucking tasty." His little nip on my skin is to tempt me into having sex with him again. Between the two of them, I'm never alone. Even though they gave me my own room.

It was their way of allowing me my space. I get my room, a huge bed and I get to invite whoever I want each night. No hard feelings if I chose to spend time with one of them at a time or bring them both in.

I just made it easy on myself and told them both to come in here every night. It's less stress on me and I'm learning that the two of them are working it out so that they get their one on one time with me.

It's a win win situation for me.

"Where's this party tonight?" Noah walks in and Levi doesn't stop his hand from sliding under my t-shirt.

"At the Ward Mansion." Levi has to work security and I've been hired to bartend. Noah notices what Levi is doing to me, so he moves to the bed quickly.

Levi's hand slides under my panties, causing me to gasp with his intrusion. "Ah, fuck." His fingers go deep, kissing my G-spot perfectly each time he moves. I shift and squirm into a frenzy of sensations, especially when Noah slides in next to me, pulling my mouth towards his. He kisses me hard, swallowing my moans while I ride through a body quivering orgasm.

One that I've grown accustomed to.

"I love you, Kali," Levi whispers against my neck as Noah finishes our kiss and I begin to come down from my high.

"I love you, too." It's something he says to me often now. Something he didn't say until they came up with the idea to share me, but something I knew he felt long before.

"I think you're all right, too." Noah makes me smile as he teases. He also tells me often. There's no shortage of love in this house and it's quickly become a place I feel at home in.

I don't know why I ever thought I could leave either one of them. The darkness I felt when I left was deafening and something I would've never recovered from. I'm destined to be with Noah and Levi. Looking back, it was obvious long ago.

It may be considered taboo to some, but I've never worried about what others think of me. I love my guys. I love my life and what it's become now that I've taken this leap of faith and followed love. Who wouldn't want two men cherishing them like these two do me?

I'm safe. I'm happy. I'm loved. What more could a girl ask for?

*Please consider reviewing this book on Amazon and Goodreads! Reviews help the book get more attention!*

# BOOKS BY HILARY STORM

Six
Seven

### Rebel Walking Series
In A Heartbeat
Heaven Sent
Banded Together
No Strings Attached
Hold Me Closer
Fighting the Odds
Never Say Goodbye
Whiskey Dreams

### Bryant Brothers Series
Don't Close Your Eyes

### Alphachat.com Series
Pay for Play
Two can Play

### Elite Forces Series
ICE
FIRE
STONE
STEELE – coming in February

## Stalk Hilary Here

Website: www.hilarystormwrites.com
Facebook: https://www.facebook.com/pages/Hilary-Storm-Author/492152230844841
Goodreads:
https://www.goodreads.com/author/show/7123141.Hilary_Stor
m?from_search=true
Twitter: @hilary_storm
Instagram: http://instagram.com/hilstorm
Snapchat: hilary_storm